SANGEETA BANDYOPADHYAY

AF767466

ekadā

AN
ASHOKA CENTRE FOR
TRANSLATION
SERIES

SANGEETA BANDYOPADHYAY

SELECTED STORIES

TRANSLATED FROM
THE BENGALI
BY SAYARI DEBNATH

ekadā

First published in English as *Sangeeta Bandyopadhyay: Selected Stories* in 2026 by Ekadā, an imprint of Westland Books, a division of Nasadiya Technologies Private Limited, with the Ashoka Centre for Translation, Ashoka University

No. 269/2B, First Floor, 'Irai Arul', Vimalraj Street, Nethaji Nagar, Alapakkam Main Road, Maduravoyal, Chennai 600095

Westland, the Westland logo, Ekadā and the Ekadā logo are the trademarks of Nasadiya Technologies Private Limited, or its affiliates.

Original copyright © Sangeeta Bandyopadhyay, 2026
Translation copyright © Sayari Debnath, 2026

ISBN: 9789379856968

10 9 8 7 6 5 4 3 2 1

This is a work of fiction. Names, characters, organisations, places, events and incidents are either products of the author's imagination or used fictitiously.

All rights reserved

Typeset by Jojy Philip

Printed at Parksons Graphics Pvt. Ltd

No part of this book may be reproduced, or stored in a retrieval system, or transmitted in any form or by any means, electronic, mechanical, photocopying, recording, or otherwise, without express written permission of the publisher.

CONTENTS

SCRIPTING SMALL REBELLIONS

Sangeeta Bandyopadhyay joins the long line of female Bengali writers who have written of the domestic space and femininity as serious literary subjects. However, she is among the few writers who are primarily interested in the condition of the modern, middle-class Bengali woman. While the early Bengali women writers were contemplating education and financial freedom in their writings, Bandyopadhyay examines the lives of women in the wake of material clarity.

In her novels, Bandyopadhyay has written extensively about the modern Kolkata woman, the push and pull between her many roles—those of a mother, a daughter, a spouse—and her renunciation of them in favour of creative and personal pursuits, such as writing, spirituality and sexual freedom. These ideas find resonance in her short stories too.

In this selection of short fiction, her protagonists are upper-class, upper-caste, urban Bengali women, some of whom are well educated and financially independent. The stories unfold in domestic spheres that are mostly devoid of typical domestic strife—there are no abusive husbands or nagging mothers-in-law. The women enjoy their wealth and social status. They are ensconced in the luxuries that city living offers and exercise freedoms that come with such security. What then can be the story of such a woman, so perfect from the outside and untouched by hardship?

And yet, social status or wealth is no salve for the fraught anxieties of womanhood. The protagonists in Bandyopadhyay's stories, mostly middle-aged, are beleaguered by questions of sexuality, ageing, beauty and public pretences. These tensions play out in their personal relationships, with lovers and husbands, friends and adversaries, in the maternal home as well as the marital home. The stories take a liberal, or rather, realistic view of marriage—there are no illusions of monogamy or a happily ever after. Divorces, widowhood, remarriages and extra-marital relationships become appendages to the married couple. In 'The Holiday' and 'Fear', the reader gets to see the 'other' woman's side of the story, which, in the author's empathetic rendition, humanises a character that is otherwise villainised. The woman, who risks stability in pursuit of love and pleasure, often gets the short end of the stick while the man looks out for his own interests. The wife and mistress compete in vain for his loyalty.

'The Bedroom' and 'Picture Perfect' are stories about starting over. While female characters are strictly at the heart of these stories, the focus zooms in and out to consider the impact of a broken relationship on the larger family. In these stories, the reader meets a widow, a young woman and the ex-wife as each tries to negotiate the changed dynamics of her family. A remarriage demands acclimating herself to a new family, dating afresh requires reigniting her belief in love, while a divorce not only jeopardises her position in the family but also her child's. A relationship might have come to an end, and with it, the rhythms of life that are often taken for granted, but as the stories show, there's always a possibility to start over, with plenty of second chances and happiness on the horizon.

'The Desire to Run Away' and 'A Happy Couple' are tragicomic stories about the desperate desire to leave the old way of life and to start anew. Sometimes, even the illusion of novelty will do. A young woman plays an elaborate game of house with an unsuspecting man in order to fight boredom. The thrill of Facebook validation compels a middle-aged woman, neglected all her life, to put on a show of prosperity and fine taste as likes and comments begin to pour in from complete strangers. Bandyopadhyay's slant sense of humour, which creeps up unwittingly, is a perfect trope for gently pointing us to the great flair we all have for drama.

The winds of change take the centrestage in 'Panchali's Lover' and 'Hallucination'. After having proved themselves loyal wives and dutiful mothers, women of advancing age confront changes they are wholly unprepared for. In 'Panchali's Lover', the untimely death of the protagonist's tailor turns into a personal tragedy when she realises that no one else has known her body as well as he. While in 'Hallucination', the relationship of the female lead's adult son makes her nervous about being replaced—she resorts to embarrassing antics to remind her future daughter-in-law that no one can take her son away.

In 'The Old Age Home', an elderly woman living in a retirement home battles everyday indignities as she bickers with her peers about food, toilets and the caregivers' attention. Though poor and abandoned, she is proud and cannot believe this is what her life has come to. A scare in the morning queue for the toilet strips her of all the dignity and pride she has, unexpectedly freeing her from her emotional cage. She decides to make the best of her remaining years.

Perhaps the most unsettling story in this collection is 'Creatures of Domesticity'. A married couple's life is upended by the wife's unexpected illness. What begins as a sombre tale of disability and marital responsibility ends on a strange, surreal note—a warning about the repercussions of codependency.

The stories are largely set in Kolkata and its immediate suburbs, and the reader sees how urban morality and aesthetics shape the lives of women. Their freedom is always double-edged. While material comforts are guaranteed, the rigid boundaries of monogamy, sexuality and family roles still prove to be an impediment to their most private desires. They often remain unfulfilled. These women are eventually forced to fit themselves into conventional moulds. A small rebellion is tolerated, but a revolution isn't.

However, it is the unexpectedness, joy and sheer daring of these small rebellions that make Bandyopadhyay's stories such a delight to read. They nudge the reader to imagine what would happen if women found a way to redefine their roles in personal and social relationships, if they lived like men, not answerable for their actions. For now, there are no answers, only stories.

Bandyopadhyay's stories are links in the long, unbroken chain of feminist solidarity, and remind the reader that they are not alone.

SAYARI DEBNATH

CREATURES OF DOMESTICITY

EARLY MORNING

Getting out of bed would mean calling her husband, so out of embarrassment and kindness, and sympathy for the sleeping, she could not leave the bed even though she wanted to. She continued to lie still as she wondered about all sorts of things. She could not get out of bed in the morning without another person's help. Another person—meaning, the man who was her husband. Who else was at home anyway? Lying down for too long made her body as stiff as wood. Meaning, she could not exert force on her hips to get up. It was not like she'd experience any kind of pain or cramps—she simply did not have the ability to stand. She couldn't even get herself to do something so simple. She'd have to be helped up. She'd prop herself up on her hands for a while and then slowly lower her feet to the ground. An attempt to stand would set her heels alight with pain. She would imagine the weight of her body splintering and crackling the bones in her ankles. Her husband would circle her with his arms as he helped her be upright. She'd look at him gratefully every morning and say, 'What would I do? What would I do? How'd I manage without you?'

The man who was her husband coaxed her to walk as he helped her take a few steps around various corners of this wall-enclosed space they called a flat. Once she demonstrated some movement, he'd take her to the bathroom, and wait outside, saying, 'Call me if you need anything.'

It took a while for this osteoporosis-related morning stiffness to go away. It'd take her an hour or two to regain control of her body. After that, she'd lean her weight against the wall and walk with a limp. Because of this, the wall bore numerous, well-detailed imprints of her palms.

Lying down, she noticed the uncovered back of the man who was her husband—there was a deep gash in it, still raw and crusted with blood. She tried to reach for the wound and stroke it in her half-conscious state. Just then, the man woke up with a start.

'How late is it?' he asked in alarm.

'Not night, not night. It's dawn, it's dawn. See, it's morning now,' she answered waving her hand.

'Oh, oh!' he said taking deep breaths as he got out of bed. He left the room. She waited for him—he was in the bathroom. She needed to go too.

The man returned after splashing water on his face. He helped her up. The water droplets clinging to his hair dripped onto her lips. She wiped them away. According to her, the smell of a person's breath seems pleasing only at first. When the feelings between two people are still new. Raw. Familiarity, intense and long-term, makes a person's breath, sweat and smell unbearable. The reason for this might be the complete knowledge of each other's bodies.

Like every day, the man helped her be steady on her feet and then took her to the balcony to rest. He went to make tea. She noticed a Matador van forcing itself into the narrow lanes of their street.

It made her listless. The Matador was bulging with furniture although there weren't too many things after all—beds and mattresses, a water filter, an almirah, a dressing table, a pull-out couch. Furniture that could be found in any home. A taxi arrived on the heels of the Matador. The door opened and a young woman stepped out with a baby on her hips. This wasn't all. Soon, a motorbike turned up too. The driver kicked the stand and parked the bike.

'Get the things from the taxi,' the young woman said to the man.

The baby started to wail. 'Go inside. I'll take care of everything,' the man told her.

'Where's the key? Give it to me.'

Holding the key tightly in her hands, the woman climbed to the first floor of the green building. She threw open the collapsible gate and walked in. They were obviously the new renters.

She hadn't seen the old renters for some time. When had they left? Perhaps it was when she was sick and confined to her bed. She could not come to the balcony during those days.

The bedroom of the first-floor flat was clearly visible from her fourth-floor balcony. The previous renters were a middle-aged man and his indecorous wife. She did not care about who was peeking into their bedroom while she changed her clothes. On many an afternoon, a middle-aged man who was not her husband could be seen entering the empty street and making his way to their flat. The curtains of the bedroom would be only half-drawn, and sitting on her chair, she had been a regular witness to the middle-aged woman and the unidentified man's aggressive, violent pouncing in bed.

She had told the man who was her husband about this quite a few times. 'You're trapped at home but at least you have no trouble passing time,' he answered.

'Even the television doesn't excite me so much,' she said.

'Oh, oh! Don't I know that.'

The kind man had lined the balcony with plants so that she could stay hidden from the world while she spied on it.

It was almost nine-thirty by the time she was done surveying the new neighbours and their attempt to set up their new home. In the meantime, she drank tea and slurped the milk and cornflakes her husband had poured out for her. She sat holding a ripe banana in her hand, though she did not feel like eating it—it was nice to look at and nicer still to hold. The Matador van was empty. The woman came out of the bedroom holding her baby and vanished somewhere inside the house. The man wiped his brow with a towel while he stood smoking a cigarette on the balcony. He had swept the house and swabbed it too. He laid the doormats at the right spots. A few domestic workers walked noisily past him in their worn-out plastic slippers. He tried to stop them. He was successful the third time.

'Let me call your Boudi. Talk to her,' he said.

It was ten o'clock in the morning. Time for the man who was her husband to leave for work. Their maid had arrived. The man who was her husband was relieved.

'Now you're her responsibility,' he said with a smile. 'She will give you your lunch. Don't forget to take a nap afterwards.

I have kept the medicines on the bed. Keep your phone close. I'll call. You should also call people, talk to them. You won't feel bored then. Don't sit in the same place for a long time, your muscles will become tense. Walk carefully when you do.'

'The bills are so expensive,' she said.

'That's okay. I'd have to spend money on going out, plays and movies, hotels and restaurants, cosmetics and so on, if you were well. But that's not the case anymore.'

They had had this conversation before. She thought it was two sides of the same coin—money would be spent one way or the other. It could either pay for doctors, hospitals and medicines or vacations, eating out and trivial purchases.

The man climbed down the stairs. She spotted him in the narrow street, he turned around to wave at her. She waved back. The man would not be visible once he stepped onto the big road. The morning would merge into the afternoon and the afternoon would give way to the evening and eventually, the night—the time when the man would return.

AFTERNOON

The maid swept the house, mopped it, and bundled her up for her afternoon bath.

'Boudi, you've become skinny like a scarecrow. You're eating well and you do nothing all day except sleep and sit. What are the doctors saying?'

The maid was a chatterbox. It did not matter if she answered her, or even listened to her, the girl went on and on without pausing for breath. 'Do you know what happened in Rasmoni Bagan?'

'They have no dearth of money—they deal in kerosene, and have oil mills and other businesses too,' the maid continued as she towelled her hair. 'The doctor accidentally killed their eldest son by injecting the wrong medicine. He is refusing to admit it, of course. But the neighbours have raided his clinic and broken everything inside it. Oh, what a scene! The morgue has just released the body. I took a look at it before coming here—it was cold and blue.'

Still chattering, the maid sat down in front of her with a long iron knife. She chopped the vegetables and dumped them on a steel plate.

'What good is money?' she said, shaking her head. 'No one can change fate. Went to the hospital for treatment and died at the hands of an expensive doctor. It's better to be poor, I have no complaints.'

'Isn't your hair still wet?' the maid exclaimed as she was about to lie down. 'Sit up for a bit, please. I'll give you rice. Shall I fry some bitter gourd too? The medicines have ruined your taste buds.'

The maid went into the kitchen to make lunch. She called the man who was her husband.

'What are you doing?'

'I'm outside. Eating cake now, will have tea later.'

'Bring some cake for me. Haven't had it in a long time.'

'I will.'

'Whom should I call today?'

'Hold on, let me think …' He tried to be of help.

She hung up and dialled another number.

'How are you feeling?' asked a woman's voice from the other end.

'The same,' she answered tearfully.

'It frightens me to think about you. We're related by blood. What if something similar happens to me? Paralysed for so many days … I wouldn't wish it on my worst enemy!'

'Yes,' she said.

'Will you never be okay again?'

'I'll only get worse, or so I've been told.'

'How did something so terrible happen to you?'

She did not want to talk about her illness, she wanted to talk about something else.

'Let it be—what about your daughter's wedding?'

'Wedding? Okay, let me tell you. She got a very odd proposal. The groom's parents are deaf and mute but the boy is completely normal. He has a very good job but I'm not sure if we should agree to it. Is it considered good luck to have deaf and mute parents-in-law? It is, as far as I'm concerned. My daughter won't have to listen to constant cribbing. Doesn't everyone want their in-laws to be like that? But what if her baby is mute and deaf too …?'

The rest of the call was spent talking about this. She started to feel drowsy soon after but decided against taking a nap. She was stuck to her spot for the entire day anyway, and if she were to sleep now, she would be awake all night. She did not mind not getting any sleep but the man would be worried—terrified even—and refuse to sleep too.

It was hot. She reached for the regulator to increase the fan's speed when the knob suddenly came off and rolled away under the almirah. She looked around her with a dumbfounded expression—there was the bed on one side and a bureau. It was impossible to lower herself in the space between the two and look for the missing knob. If only there were some other way. She needed to put it back on the regulator and increase the fan's speed. She was feeling very hot. However, her body could not be subjected to such exertion. All of a sudden, the wish to crumple and tuck herself into the narrow space hit her with a tremendous force. She started to pant and flail her arms aimlessly. She let out a deep breath and lay down again on the bed. Tears streamed down her face.

She dialled another number and enquired, 'So what did you make for lunch today?'

It was her long-time friend on the other side. Rest assured, she was never irritated by her calls. She had cooked two vegetarian dishes. No sooner did she hear about it than she called her maid.

'Can't you cook the vegetables nicely?' she asked. 'All I can taste is onion, garlic, ginger and some more onion, garlic, ginger. I don't want the same thing every day.'

She ordered the maid to look for the regulator knob right away. Still on the phone, she noticed the maid dragging out clumps of dirt from under the almirah as she hunted for the missing knob. It was obvious that the maid was a slacker, a good-for-nothing.

'This city has become unliveable,' her friend continued speaking from the other side. 'I was so happy in Mumbai. There's no work culture here. The tap is not working properly and I have been tearing my hair out trying to get the plumber to fix it. He promises to turn up but never does! On top of that, his phone is always switched off! He says his mother is unwell or his son has loose motions. What a liar! He found a live-in maid for me—a cousin apparently—but turns out she is his girlfriend. I fired her on the spot. Why pretend your girlfriend is your cousin?'

'Do you really not like this city?' she asked.

She did not hear her friend's answer—at that moment, her heart fled from her crippled body to wander around the city's busy marketplaces. She was wearing a nice saree and walking around the streets with no difficulty. There was no one with her. The streets were lined with clothing shops and the mannequins were draped in gorgeous sarees. The hawkers crowded the footpaths and sold all kinds of fabrics and clothes. The tramlines zigzagged on the roads. She did not know that these tracks were a relic from a different time and trams had disappeared from this part of the city. She could hear the tram bells ringing amid the din of buses, cars and autorickshaws. The everyday sounds of honking and people arguing sounded like the music of a long-awaited festival. The calls of 'Boudi! Didi!' from the hawkers delighted her. They needed her and she felt grateful for the attention. She came out of her stupor. She realised how desperately she needed the man who was her husband. She was no better than a vegetable—he fed her, looked after her, kept her alive. He did not burden her with any responsibilities.

She hung up and immediately called her husband.

'Everything that you do for me, do you do it out of fear?'

'No, not at all! Who will look after you if not me?'

'Do you like to take care of me every minute of every day? Don't you hate it sometimes?'

'What are you even saying? Had lunch? Take a nap. Get some rest.'

'Is this what the rest of my life will be like?'

'It's not a problem, is it? Unless I die without warning! Who will look after you then?'

The maid returned to the room. She had finished cooking. 'Let's eat,' she said, 'You won't be able to manage on your own.'

She refused. The maid placed the bowls of rice, daal and vegetables on the dining table and left. She struggled to the table and put away the food. She lay down again and turned on the television. The channel was broadcasting news about the man who could fly. A wing-like contraption was mounted on his back and the man jumped from a tall cliff somewhere. Flapping his wings, he landed on the ground like a big bird. It appeared as though the man was as light as a feather. He felt no pain, nothing could hurt him—he stood victorious on the cliff as he smiled beatifically at the rest of humankind, smug in his achievement.

She wondered if it was true. Or was she imagining things? She could not stand, walk or run … but perhaps one day she could fly. She could fly wherever her heart desired. She would defy gravity and then fly right towards it. But wouldn't she fall and hurt herself?

Still lost in thought, she called the man who was her husband.

'I'm with a client. Calling you back,' he whispered.

The light began to fade while she waited for the call and before she knew it, it was dark.

EVENING

The maid came back in the evening to give her tea and sweep the house one more time. She fetched the dry clothes from the verandah and folded them before leaving. On some evenings, if she felt like it, she ordered the maid to get crispy kochuris or shingaras from the roadside sweet shop. Every evening, without fail, a squirrel climbed up to her third-floor verandah for some unknown reason. It foraged in the plants on the balcony, jumped from one pot to another, and nibbled at something or other. The man who was her husband had tied a bell to a plant for the guest. It rang every time the squirrel jumped at it. On the evenings that she ate kochuri or shingara, she scattered the crumbs all over the balcony for it and on the other days, biscuits. She had not eaten lunch today but she did not feel hungry. She had asked the man who was her husband to bring her some cake. He definitely would. If he didn't, or if he forgot, she would pick a fight with him. She wished for a terrible misunderstanding between them so that she could fight with him and tell him off with some choice words. The fight would escalate to a point where she would storm out of the flat limping. She would stand at the top of the stairs and, in a fit of rage, lose her balance, tumble all the way down and die. But the man never lost his temper. They had coexisted for a long time and he got old, then bald, but she had not once seen him get angry. These days, his eyes revealed nothing but a deep fear. He was so scared that he had given up standing upright and preferred to crawl around. Perhaps he was afflicted by the same malady as her. She had spoken to him on the phone just a while ago.

'Sorry, sorry, don't mind me. A pain-in-the-ass client. But what can I do? I had to hear him out.' How apologetic he sounded.

'Everyone wants to be young for as long as they can,' she said. 'There are so many ways to prevent ageing these days.

Plastic surgery to keep the skin elastic. Researchers are looking at ways to keep the body young and alert. But will you see if there's a way to get old quickly? Has anyone discovered a way? For instance, a medicine that will age a person by ten years overnight, another ten the next night and so on until in a week the body is in a state of total disrepair and beyond the scope of any treatment. So, you have no choice but to submit to death the next morning. Something like this?'

'And if one were to take several pills on a night, then their body would turn to dust almost immediately?'

'Yes, yes, exactly!'

The man who was her husband was quiet for a few moments. She did not notice the night had grown thick around her and the squirrel had long vanished.

'Your eyes are glistening,' she said.

'No, no, no, no. Not at all,' the man protested mournfully. 'I'm just trying to understand you. Understand? Do you understand?'

NIGHT

It started to rain around eight in the evening. Tired from watching serials on television, she was getting increasingly irritable when the man who was her husband arrived drenched to the skin.

'Cake?' she asked.

'I've got it. Relax.'

She sighed exasperatedly.

'Tell me the truth,' she asked. 'Your eyes were glistening, weren't they?'

The man's downturned lashes covered his eyes. His grey, insensate eyes.

'It's very important for you to get better. Very, very important,' he said looking hesitatingly at her with his dull, grey eyes. 'To go out on the streets, meet some people … or you'll go mad.'

She did not let the man change out of his wet clothes. The man did not dare ask if they could talk after he had changed his clothes.

'Mad?' she screamed, 'So you've been talking about me? You're getting tired of me, aren't you?'

'No, no, not at all,' said the man plaintively. 'I want you to get well. I want to take you to Darjeeling, Madhya Pradesh, Kashmir, Goa!'

'Will you no longer be scared if I'm well again?'

The man lowered his head at this question. She let him go and made her way to the balcony again. Her eyes were glued to the bedroom of the new neighbours. The woman came in, looked for something and went out. Next, the husband and the wife walked into the room together talking companionably.

The man who was her husband served dinner a little later. She could not comb her hair, her fingers felt very stiff, so the man combed and tied it for her. He also swept away the strands of hair that had fallen on the floor.

Much later, they turned off the lights and lay down next to each other. 'Go to sleep,' she said.

'No, you first.'

'Why?'

'You just took medicines to calm the nerves. Don't talk so much.'

'Do you think they do what they claim?'

He sat up.

'What do you mean? Don't they?'

'Just say yes or no. Don't I sleep like a log? I slump, don't I? You keep moving my legs and arms all night long.'

The man was quiet. She started to cry.

'You still don't believe that I don't do it by choice!'

She shook her head furiously—that was all the movement she could muster with her paralysed body.

'I don't like sucking your blood, you must believe me. I have no control over my pain or health. My teeth are not so sharp that I can bite you. Why don't you understand?'

'But I've seen the pool of blood on the corner of your lips.'

The man was scared.

Her eyes glowed.

'What did you say?'

'No, no. So what! I am not complaining. I have only one request. The wound refuses to heal if blood is sucked from the same spot.'

She turned away.

'I'm feeling sleepy. I have to survive tomorrow. You too.'

She was sobbing.

'Why don't you use a good ointment? You too have the right to live. Just like me.'

PANCHALI'S LOVER

The ladies' tea party started at half past four in the afternoon. Panchali stepped into the club at exactly forty minutes past four. She gently pushed open the door to the Blue Room. She adjusted the end of her saree with one hand while the other rested firmly on the thick strap of her designer handbag. Many club members, nearly a hundred of them, were surprised when she came in. And some others expressed enchantment and distaste in equal measure. The distaste was from those who were closer to Panchali in age. They were all older than fifty-five and for the last thirty-seven years, they had been comparing themselves with her. They noticed how Panchali had been getting on in age just like them but did not have a single strand of grey hair to show for it. There were no wrinkles on her skin, no folds of flab clinging to her back, no slacking belly, no sad-looking, saggy breasts. Their breasts were somehow made to hold up and appear firm. But her breasts were the same as they were thirty-seven years ago when she first stepped into the club with her parents-in-law, as a young bride, barely twenty. Although Panchali didn't look as young anymore, they resented the fact that age had made them lethargic while she bloomed like a bud in spring. She dressed as she pleased and worse still, looked ravishing each time.

You couldn't accuse them of not taking care of themselves. They did everything Panchali did: swimming, steam baths, sauna sessions, body massages, colouring their hair with henna, facials, threading, waxing, manicure, pedicure—the lot! They took vitamin tablets too. They flaunted their expensive sarees and jewellery. Carefully picked their accessories and wore generous amounts of make-up and perfumes. And laughed with abandon. Their days were an endless stream of events, functions, ladies' meets, kitty parties, card games, gambling, flower shows, dog shows, carnivals, musicals, dinners, lunches and so on.

After all, this was the most elite club in eastern India. The colonial rules and regulations were still in place and strictly followed. The women members of the club were the crème de la crème of society. Therefore, such engagements and activities were a regular part of their lives and could not be dismissed as an extravagance or an affectation.

Nevertheless, no one was as beautiful as Panchali. There was no dearth of beautiful women in the club—so glamorous they appeared to be of royal birth, some looking like dolls freshly plucked from a glass box. Some were so delicate that new sarees pricked their skin; and they hired people to wear their new clothes and break them in. A lifetime of luxury had left a glorious sheen on their skin—and yet, they appeared utterly dull and unremarkable next to Panchali.

It was hard to say what made Panchali unique. Was it her height? Complexion? Facial features? Hair? Eyes? Teeth? The way she turned her head? Sat? Stood? Walked? Her physique?

Her mannerisms? Intelligence? Behaviour? Sartorial sense? The way she draped her saree? Or her blouse?

B-l-o-u-s-e?

However strange it may sound, a blouse is a woman's best friend. It's true! It gives generously and takes away ruthlessly too. Would Pratibha Patil look her part as the first female president of India without the blouses she wore? Then there was Mandira Bedi, who was practically unrecognisable without her spaghetti-strap ones. In red-light districts, the whores wear nothing besides blouses and petticoats, and their garishly coloured blouses are enough to give away their trade. The women who worry about the day's lunch invitations, coffee meets, kitty parties on the roof of some industrialist's house, piano or sitar recitals at exclusive venues, corporate dinners at five-star hotels and housewarming parties know that blouses cannot be trifled with.

Women who woke up and put the kettle on to boil, chopped vegetables and marinated the fish with salt and turmeric, cooked and tempered the daal, folded the mosquito nets, helped the school-, college- and office-goers in their family get ready, and then somehow managed to take a quick shower, slip their feet into the nearest pair of sandals, grab an umbrella and rush to catch the bus to the schools where they taught or banks where they counted other people's money, and again, jostled their way into cramped buses, trams, metros in the evenings, bought beguni or aloo'r chop from the neighbourhood snack shop, made themselves a strong cup of milk tea before finally putting up their feet and watching their daily soap, did not accord a blouse the same importance as did Panchali and her fellow women club members. Ordinary women bought blouses from roadside shops and were happy as long as they matched the colour of their saree. As for weddings and other events, they would simply cover their backs with the end of the saree to hide the sorry state of their blouse. They could of course get blouses stitched by the neighbourhood tailor—perhaps it wouldn't fit snugly at the shoulders, or the neckline would look clumsy, or the tailor would make the blouse so ill-fitting that the bra (cups, straps and everything else) would be visible to everyone. The missing hook would be replaced with a safety pin and the black blouse that was paired with sarees of every style and colour would fade with use. Yet, they held on to these, treating them like fine lingerie while their special blouses were stuffed into bags and put away.

If you doubt the truth of this statement, then I urge you to step into the club during the Bijoya Dashami congregations or the evening get-togethers on Poila Boishakh. The club is stuffed to its gills on those days and beautiful women are buzzing all over. They glow like the diamonds, pearls and gems they adorn themselves with. What was not possible in any corner of the earth happened regularly here, and it was a sight that bedazzled everyone—nearly two thousand and five hundred women draped in sarees circled the rooms in a blinding haze. Their bodies radiated light. The tinkle of laughter and the clinking of the trays bearing betel leaves and other offerings to the goddess rang in unison with the clinking of their jewellery. The heavy silk drapes blew gently in the breeze and the tall trees shielded them from the harsh sunlight. The bearers—old, turbaned, with kohl-lined eyes—stood by silently waiting for instructions. The dirty, confusing city disappeared at the horizon, as though this was where the world ended—nothing beyond this room needed to exist. The chosen ones had made the journey to this heavenly abode and they could finally rest peacefully. The women, wrapped in fine, expensive sarees were here to stay. No other place in the world was worthy of their presence. These angels sent from heaven would be here till the end of time—floating in the air and laughing melodiously. A new dawn was never to come; this evening would last forever.

Needless to say, the bodies of the two thousand and five hundred women were adorned with two thousand and five hundred types of blouses and each of them appeared familiar in some way or other.

However, if there was one woman who stood out in this congregation of two thousand and five hundred angels, it was Panchali. It seemed that Panchali hadn't picked the blouse but the blouse had made a pilgrimage from the heavens to adorn her ethereal body.

Therefore, Panchali always arrived ten minutes late. She wanted every eye in the club to reflect her radiance. No one could ignore her once she arrived—indeed, they looked at her with absolute devotion. Of course, some old-timers frowned disapprovingly.

'You look fantastic! Which boutique did you buy the saree from? Which tailor designed your blouse? How well it fits!' one of the newbies inevitably gushed.

Not once had Panchali's blouse concealed the contours of her beautiful body—every crease, fold and curve was on display for admiration and envy.

And today, when she pushed open the doors to the Blue Room and entered in a black Dhakai saree embellished with black embroidery, the rest of them had to face the truth yet again.

Panchali wore a saree for the first time when she was only seventeen years old. Many, many years had passed since then. She had scoured every corner of the planet for the most elegant, unique and expensive sarees. She now had innumerable sarees. Yet, those sarees were of little value without the right blouses. She had so many blouses designed for her over the years that it was impossible to keep count. In addition to that, every blouse of hers was the handiwork of the same tailor. She was loyal to a tailoring shop at Rashbehari Junction. She had walked from Rowland Road to Rashbehari Junction a few thousand times for this very purpose and not once were her efforts in vain. The blouses fit her like a second skin, every single time. She never had to waste time getting the blouses remade. There was never a problem with the design, measurements or fittings. For nearly half a century, the tailor had faithfully served her family. First, Panchali's mother and then, her. But something unusual happened today.

Panchali had picked out a saree for the ladies' meet but she couldn't wear it after all. She had sent her driver to collect thirteen new blouses from My Lady, her reliable tailors. They were made to match her various crepe, georgette, Maheshwari and Chanderi sarees. She shut the door to her dressing room and tried on the blouses no sooner than the driver handed them over. The first one she wore was a turquoise blue Dhakai blouse. Her reflection in the mirror baffled her. She quickly tried on the rest of them until finally, she beat her forehead in exasperation. None of them fit!

Not only that, but every blouse looked shabbily made, the cups of both breasts were of incorrect sizes, some were so tight she could not breathe while the others were so loose that they bunched up awkwardly. The neckline rested in an ugly manner on her cleavage.

What the fuck had happened? It was a disaster. The blouses were cut from the same fabric as the sarees. She would not find them in any shop. There was no solution. Her sarees were totally unwearable without the right blouses.

She went into the bedroom and flung herself on the bed. Nothing like this had happened before, so why now? It was a disaster, and she began to mourn loudly. As far as she was concerned, it was as if the tailor had slashed her arms and disfigured her for life.

Panchali was enchanting and her beauty beyond comparison. She was as graceful as a fawn, her face was the same shape as a betel leaf, her limbs were taut and long, her waist was still slim, her behind was shapely, and her stomach was as flat as ever. The only exception to her long, reedy physique was her succulent, pendulous breasts. They were still full and firm, and thrilling to look at. Since her days as a young girl and then a young woman, her breasts had charmed hundreds of men, perhaps more. Panchali knew that the waist or ass did not merit much attention but the gift of beautiful breasts should not go unappreciated. For her part, she had always been grateful for them.

Panchali had never experienced such overwhelming grief. She took a shower, put on a black Dhakai saree, tied her hair, rubbed some lipstick on her mouth and consoled her weeping heart by assuring it that all its troubles would vanish as soon as she stepped into My Lady. There must have been a mistake; that was all there was to it. Gouri-di would take care of everything. These were the thoughts swirling in her head as she drove to the club. Once she was there, she got busy chatting, singing, and having a good time. The tragedy from a few hours ago was forgotten.

It was six thirty in the evening and the party was still on. The chatter usually died down after two cups of tea or coffee. The women split themselves into different groups and talked energetically about their lives. The party always started with a game of Housie and the gossip passed liberally from one lip to another. Mallika was missing, meaning she'd be the victim of their loose tongues today. Panchali's son, Udit, was to get married in a few weeks and there was a lot of talk about it too. The would-be bride's trousseau was being designed by Luthra, a famous Mumbai-based fashion designer who was charging a whopping two and a half lakh rupees for it! Panchali was having a great time reeling off the names of stores and designers she was shopping from and the audience eagerly clung to her words. They weren't just listening but also reminiscing about the weddings of their children, the lavish gifts that were exchanged, and the treasures discovered in the trunks of their long-dead grandmothers. It suddenly occurred to Panchali that My Lady would close at seven. She sprang up from her chair, waved a quick goodbye, and almost sprinted to Rashbehari Junction. On her way in the car, she rehearsed the lines she would say to Gouri-di, including how she would say them so that Gouri-di could put her out of her misery without further delay.

Panchali was married into a family of excess. They ate lavishly, went on exotic vacations, held get-togethers and parties, and hosted musical recitals. It was a grand life. One evening, she would wear a black zari saree, tuck a rose into her hair, and swim in the waves of Dhrupad music; on another evening, she would wear her expensive chiffon saree and dance late into the night to the loud beats of rock 'n' roll. She excelled in the art of showing off her shapely body and her husband was not one to object. Moreover, in their circles, this is how women flaunted their status.

In fact, her husband, Alok, hated it if she repeated her outfits. Hence, she wore halter neck blouses, blouses that had strings or bows instead of hooks, skimpy blouses and blouses with deep necklines. A blouse worn once was never repeated. She had not been able to savour the delicious attention while Udit was a child. But once he came into his own, Panchali became the cause of envy of every woman who laid eyes on her. As she grew older, she became even more sprightly and radiant. Truly indomitable. It went without saying that her blouses continued to play the most important role in refining her beauty.

Many years ago, when she went to college or stepped out on the street, men would stop in their tracks to gaze at her chest.

'You're built just like your grandmother, Panchali,' her mother had remarked once. 'She breastfed eleven babies but see what her breasts look like even at this age?'

In fact, even the professors at college could not turn their eyes away from the fine saree covering her chest. Neither were her uncles indifferent to her charms. She was so shy as a young girl! Like carefully unwrapping a precious but fragile gift, Alok had undressed her on their wedding night and pretty much lost his mind after seeing her uncovered breasts for the first time. What she remembered from their first time together was how timid she used to be! However, she was not a shy girl for much longer. She soon experienced—and relished—the taste of being the reason for many a woman's envy. There was great fun in flirting and the adulation was the reason for her happiness. But did that mean she had no other weapon in her arsenal besides her delicious breasts? No, not at all. She was well-mannered and soft-spoken, made friends easily, spoke elegantly, and was intelligent too. Still, it would be foolish to deny that her physical beauty played a big role in her self-confidence.

My Lady, the tailoring shop, was divided into two sections. The customer had to walk up to the upper floor to get their measurements taken and try on the clothes, while the ground floor was reserved for the delivery of orders. Panchali climbed upstairs carrying a large bag.

'Gouri-di!' she exclaimed as soon as she saw her, sounding like a person at sea.

'Gouri-di!' had been employed at the shop for nearly fifty years. It took Panchali no less than two hours to place her order. She chatted with the workers, drank many cups of tea and asked about the well-being of other customers. She was an asset to the shop and was treated with deference. By now, Gouri-di had become as important to her as family and she made sure to gift her a saree for Pujo every year. Over seventy years old, slim, tall, with bobbed hair, Gouri-di was a permanent fixture at the shop. She had no dearth of stories to tell Panchali. Sitting on her seat year after year, she had seen and spoken with many important and well-known women. Actresses at their peak, advocates, judges, barristers, surgeons, dancers and wives of filthy rich businessmen. Not a single name was missing from her list of clients. Each of these ladies had distinct demands about how their blouses should be made and each of them had their own understanding of which blouse to pair with what saree.

'I have seen how tastes and dressing sense change with one's lifestyle,' Gouri-di had often told Panchali. As a regular visitor to the shop, Panchali, too, had witnessed this.

A woman who was devoted to the stern neckline of the air hostess-style blouse would suddenly demand one day, 'I want a deep-cut blouse. Don't want to hide my cleavage anymore. Make the back so wide that nothing except the straps of the bra is hidden.' She had fallen in love with a young man and had become a pain in the ass for her elderly husband and her adult sons and daughters.

Panchali had witnessed the opposite too. A wife had caught her husband red-handed with another woman. So, she got rid of her saree, the sacred vermilion, and the red and white bangles signifying her married status. She cut her hair short and adopted the modern outfits of skirts, tops and denim pants. A complete makeover. This is how she marked her protest. She was old and the only way to kick out the mistress was by changing how she looked. Gouri-di had been a useful confidant in this matter. Her long years of experience at the shop had not just made her an excellent tailor, but also a skilful storyteller.

'What's wrong?' asked Gouri-di when she detected the distress in Panchali's voice.

'What are these blouses you have made, Gouri-di?' she asked, putting her bag down with a thud. 'None of them fit me and don't even get me started on the necklines! These are not my measurements at all! Thirteen blouses and all of them messed up. Nothing like this has ever happened before!'

There were five or seven women of different ages in the room with Gouri-di and Panchali—and their eyes sprang wide open with curiosity.

'Imtiaz died last Thursday. A sudden pain in his chest. Everything was over in two hours. Not just you but many women's blouses will suffer the same fate.'

'Imtiaz? Imtiaz is dead?' Panchali slumped down on the wooden stool. He did look very old and frail the last time she saw him. Gouri-di's measurements and Imtiaz's tailoring—the winning team that designed her blouses! That very same Imtiaz was dead?

'He's dead! There was magic in his hands,' someone tutted from the back.

'Goes without saying. He was our biggest star,' agreed Gouri-di. 'He would sit in his corner, puff on beedis and stitch all day. The old man's heart must've shrunk with exertion.'

'Does that mean Imtiaz didn't stitch my blouses?' interrupted Panchali.

'No. His son Sukhi Ali did.'

'It's clear he knows nothing. Why are you accepting this shoddy work, Gouri-di?'

'Why do you suppose?' Gouri-di sighed deeply and answered. 'He's only eighteen or nineteen. The youngest of Imtiaz's seven sons. None of his brothers was interested in becoming tailors, so Imtiaz took it upon himself to teach his trade to Sukhi Ali. If only his father had been around for a few more days … then he too would've become a very fine tailor.

Anyway, that was not to be. We told him that he was free to refuse orders but he didn't pay any heed to that. He said he would do it—in fact, he did one or two quite well. But now it's clear that he hasn't learnt how to tackle silk and crepe … As if it's so easy!'

A terrible weight settled on Panchali's heart. Gouri-di began emptying the big bag of its contents.

'Pujo is around the corner and the complaints will start to come in any day now. We don't have enough tailors. Who's going to take care of all the demands for alterations? Can't even run to Imtiaz now. Anyway, let me call Reba. I'll tell her to cancel the rest of Sukhi Ali's orders.' She paused for a moment.

'There's no earning member in their family right now, Panchali,' Gouri-di continued. 'If the boy knew his work well, he would easily be able to take care of his mother, sister and himself. None of Imtiaz's other sons looks after them.'

Gouri-di's words did not enter Panchali's ears. She was deep in thought.

'Gouri-di, Imtiaz made my blouses all these years, didn't he?' she asked, finally breaking her silence.

'Yes, we never gave them to anyone else.'

'So, who will make my blouses now?'

'No matter who it is, it'll be difficult to find someone as good as Imitiaz,' said Gouri-di, smiling. 'He was an artist. But why are you so worried? You can get your blouses altered if there's any problem. They'll fit you perfectly, I promise. Nothing is impossible. Just try them on before taking them home.'

Panchali nodded her head faintly but she could do nothing about the tempest brewing in her heart. No one could understand what she was going through.

'How are the wedding preparations coming along?' asked Gouri-di. 'Getting the bride's blouses made by a fashion designer, are you?'

'Let's see. I might come here,' Panchali answered, folding the alteration slip. She stood up to leave.

'I'll go now, Gouri-di. I have taken so much of your time.'

Panchali gingerly climbed down the narrow stairway. It was impossible to think about her son's wedding, and all of a sudden, her heart crumpled up in terrible sorrow. She could not accept that the person who, behind the scenes, had beautified her most prized assets with utmost dedication and care for so many years, was no longer alive. Like a discontented artist, he departed one day leaving everything behind, never to come back. He didn't even give her a chance to thank him or convey her gratitude!

Wasn't Imtiaz among the many men who crowded Panchali's life? Had she not let his graceful, artistic hands tend to her without ever really knowing him? Not just Imtiaz, she had lost a lot more. Once home, she closed the door to her bedroom and stood in front of the mirror.

'Can't I find a way to thank Imtiaz for all he has done for me? If only I could find a job for Sukhi Ali,' she thought, removing her saree.

Panchali would not be deterred. She found the whereabouts of Imtiaz's young son and brought him home with her one afternoon. Sukhi Ali, who was indeed very young, his moustache had not properly sprouted yet, was very frightened when he saw Panchali's regal mansion and stylish cars. She pulled the boy into her bedroom and slammed the door behind them. In a cooing voice, she invited him to sit on the bed and allowed him a brief moment to settle down.

'Your father was very dear to me and that's why you should treat me like your own,' she said. 'Look at me. Don't be afraid.'

She took off her saree, unhooked her bra, and let her breasts free. The curtains of the windows were drawn tightly, yet a narrow stream of light filtered into the room. Amid the light and shadow, she stood with her naked breasts parted to the sides.

'Don't be afraid,' she said again. 'Take a good look at them. You have to make blouses, not just for me but for scores of women. It's very difficult work. Your father was very good at it. You have to be too. Otherwise, Imtiaz won't be able to rest in peace.

'Look at them, don't feel shy. Touch them if you must. Show them some love. How will you make blouses if you don't learn how to love them? You don't know anything about breasts, do you? You have no idea what to do, do you?

'From now on, before you start stitching a blouse, imagine a woman standing naked in front of you. Do you understand? Sukhi Ali, you must learn to draw with needles what you see in front of you. Won't you be able to do it? Sukhi Ali, won't you be an artist just like your father, Imtiaz?'

THE HOLIDAY

What time was it? Instead of looking at the watch, I parted the heavy drapes of the window and looked outside. I saw the same scene every day—black plants shooting up from the parted lips of hell. My eyes looked into the distance as they criss-crossed the empty spaces between the trees. They finally stopped on the unknown horizon where the mountaintops were dotted with faint lights.

My eyes were searching for something new. They were not watching the mountains in the silent, oppressive darkness in vain. They would be richly rewarded for it one day. One day, they would no longer tire of seeing the same sights and would form a precious friendship with the mountains, gorges, valleys, and the clouds that gathered in the night sky.

I would grow fond of the trees and flowers too. The conifers, pine trees, cypress trees; the thick twines whose names I did not know and could not make out one from the other, but who tumbled into my heart and wound themselves around it as soon as the darkness set in. Not just the twines, but almost every tree here raised its head to the sky. The twelve-foot-wide trunks of these trees were almost always damp. Their black bark, the canopies, stringy roots and the secrets that were hidden between the leaves filled my heart with a strange fear. It had been almost a year since I had arrived amidst the mountains and the thick cover of trees. Still, I was yet to become accustomed to them.

For the last two days, the sun had been shining generously on the mountains. It was the month of May—the most fantastic time of the year here. The last two nights were not cold at all. Just one blanket was enough. In fact, I had sat on the balcony till ten o'clock last night wearing nothing but a sweater and a light shawl. The red fruits of the huge tree in front of me split open and released their seeds into the air. I loved the sound and I am quite sure I would agree to sit on the balcony if I could hear it just one more time.

Before dusk, Alomita and I had walked all the way down from the mountains to the Mall. We got cakes, bread and cookies from Glenary's and stopped for vegetables on our way back. We bought potatoes, beetroots, carrots, beans and a handful of fruits. Alomita's basket was heavier than mine. Her family comprised her husband, Adrish, and their daughter, Bhor. Her mother-in-law was to visit her in a day or two. The end of winter had prompted family and friends to make the journey to the mountains. My mother would turn up any day too, but for now, I shopped for myself.

We did not walk back like we usually did. We hired a cab. He dropped us off at the school gate for seventy rupees. We split the fare equally. Adrish-babu taught the senior students and had a flat right next to the boys' dormitory on the second floor of the main building. He was also the housemaster there.

I lived some distance away from the main building. My flat was beyond the junior wing, past the classrooms for the seventh and eighth grades and the laboratories. It was on the third floor. Alomita and I parted ways after crossing the gigantic playground. She turned to the right while I kept to the left.

Evenings in Darjeeling are very tedious. I remembered my childhood summer vacations in the hills with my parents. Then too, I got terribly bored once the sun set. Back then, there were no cable connections or televisions in the hotel rooms. And now I live here all year round. I am an art teacher at this boarding school. The drawing rooms in the furnished quarters of the school are fitted with a flat-screen TV. There's cable connectivity too. Besides, the cell phone is always tucked tightly into our palms and the computers have internet connectivity. Though it is still very boring, I no longer mind it very much.

Jalapahar, where I live, is an independent hill much higher up than Mall Road and its exclusivity sometimes made me feel lonelier than I was. It is possible that with time I will get used to the monotony. Perhaps there will come a time when I will not be able to imagine life without this apartment with a hardwood floor, the blue-and-green mountain peaks that stretched as far as my eyes could see, the pitch-black nights, the tangle of trees, the endless emptiness I felt, and the biting cold. For now, I was acutely aware of how nature was penetrating my fine skin little by little every day.

I finish dinner by eight in the evening. My maid Shanta comes from the settlement at the foothills. She is Nepali and the same age as me. She prepares the dough for ruti. I make two or three rutis for dinner. I don't like fish or meat. On most days, I try out a new recipe of daal and vegetables, and have my meals piping hot. The rest of the evening is spent reading books, watching television and emailing. I wake up at five o'clock every morning but I hate going to bed before midnight. I find myself in a constant tussle with the environment around me from nine o'clock till I fall asleep.

After returning from the Mall Road, I made rajma and a curry with raw papaya and dried lentil dumplings. My mother had packed the dumplings for me before I returned to the hills in March. There wasn't much of it. I hoped my mother would bring some more when she came. I should remind her. After dinner, I put the milk to boil. I was thinking of wrapping myself snugly and sitting on the balcony when my cell phone started to ring. Everyone in Kolkata knew this was the best time to talk to me.

The phone was on the dining table.

'It's Nandini!'

'How's it going?' I asked.

Nandini's voice made its way to me through the din behind her.

'Guess where I am?' she asked excitedly.

'Where?'

What a strange question. No how-are-you, nothing—just this dismembered question.

'In the train!'

'Oh. Where to?'

'To you.'

Nandini was coming here!

'Which train?'

'Darjeeling Express. What else?'

I was utterly confused. Nandini was on her way here. She hadn't informed me beforehand but she was already on the train. Which meant she had booked the ticket quite some time ago. That train was packed like sardines this time of the year. Even the last-minute ticket would have to be bought at least five days in advance. Then why hadn't Nandini said anything to me? Was she coming alone? Were her husband and child accompanying her?

I was slightly irritated. It would be a different matter if it were just her. My flat was compact but I could make space for one friend. Especially if she happened to be my best friend. Moreover, I had plenty of time on my hands and it would not be a problem if I wanted to spend it with Nandini or someone else. I tried to smile.

'Are you really coming or are you fucking with me?'

'I am, for real! I'm calling you from the train.'

'You're totally mad. Why didn't you tell me before? What if I wasn't here?'

'I wanted to. But I did not know if I would be able to. A lot has happened. I'll tell you about it when I'm there!' Nandini's voice trembled with excitement. What had happened?

'Are Debdutta and your son coming?'

'No,' she replied after a small pause.

'It's just you?'

'Hmm.'

It did not sound like Nandini was speaking the truth. She was not coming here by herself. Who was with her?

'I'll be there by noon. Will you be home then?' she asked.

'No. Lunch is at twelve-thirty. I have to eat lunch in the junior wing all week. I'll be home around one o'clock.'

'Then?'

'Call me when you reach the cantonment. The maid will be there. I'll tell her to let you in.'

'Thank God. See you tomorrow then! I'll hang up now.'

Nandini and I had grown up in the same neighbourhood. We had been friends for many years. She was coming to visit me. All of a sudden, I was overcome with emotions.

'Call me when you arrive at New Jalpaiguri station.'

'I will. Goodnight.'

Not at noon; my phone rang exactly at twelve-thirty. The matron, Mrs Bagchi, and I were about to enter the dining hall after ushering the last of the boys inside.

'Are you here?'

'Yes. What now?'

'Cross the big playground and then take a left. The boys are strolling around, ask any of them to point to Ms Dutta's place. Tell them you're looking for the house where Shanta works.'

'What time are you coming?'

'In half an hour.'

I told Mrs Bagchi that my childhood friend had come to visit.

'The next few days will be a lot of fun,' she said cheerfully.

'I went to the market yesterday but I did not know she was coming,' I said smiling. 'If I did, I would have at least shopped properly and bought some eggs for her. You know I don't eat them!'

It was nearly twenty past one before I returned home. It was quite hot and I was feeling energised. I decided to tell Shanta to make some coffee. We would have a nice chat while drinking it. Thankfully, I was not needed at the school before half past four.

I rang the bell. Shanta opened the door with a big smile.

'*Woh log aa gaye!*' The guests have arrived, she informed me in Hindi.

Woh log? So, it was not just Nandini. My eyes fell on the women's sandals and men's black boots in the narrow doorway. Was Debdutta here?

'Where are they?' I asked Shanta as I walked towards the drawing room.

'In the room.'

The room Shanta pointed to was my study. That was where my mother stayed when she visited me. It also doubled up as the guest bedroom. The bed was three feet wide. Big enough for one person.

The door to the study was shut.

Should I knock? Why didn't Nandini tell me Debdutta was coming? What if she were here with another man? She didn't even say hello to me and her door was already shut? I was standing in my home and was at a total loss about what I should be doing. Should I call her? Or should I retreat into my room and wait for her to come out?

I went into my room anxiously and with great discomfort, called Nandini on her cell phone. This was the only way to preserve our dignity and save us from embarrassment. The phone kept ringing. I could hear the ringtone going off in the other room but Nandini did not bother to pick up.

What was she up to? I was furious at her vulgarity. How dare she bring someone into my house without my permission and worse still, lock herself away in a room with him with such impudence? I called her again. Then once more. Then one more time. This time, she finally picked up. She answered lazily, 'Sorry, Konkona. I'll be out in a minute.'

'What do you mean by sorry? Who else is with you? Debdutta?'

'I'll be there. Just a moment!'

A man and woman spoke between themselves and then one of them went into the washroom. I heard the sound of the flush being pulled. A few moments later, Nandini's hand pushed open the door to my room. She had hastily put on a housecoat over a camisole and her hair was in a mess. I wrinkled my brows and bit hard on the inside of my cheeks to stop myself from saying something reckless. She smiled at me widely and flung herself onto my bed. She started to moan softly while rubbing her face into the bed sheet.

'What's going on, Nandini?'

'Nothing. Tirtha is here with me!'

'Tirtha? Who's that?'

'*Our* Tirtha, Konkona!'

'Tirtha?'

'Yes!'

'I don't get what you're saying. Tirtha! After so many years?'

Tirtha used to live in the same neighbourhood as us. The neighbourhood where I don't live anymore and neither does Nandini. Tirtha had left a long time but he was friends with both of us. Nandini had cried for many days after he left to study in Kanpur. She had just fallen in love with him. However, as far as I know, that affair was nipped in the bud. Tirtha was not in touch with Nandini and I did not know anything about his new life either. So how had he turned up in her life nearly fourteen or fifteen years later?

Nandini turned around and lay on her back. She smiled at my question as though she was emerging from a trance. It wouldn't be absurd for me to assume that she was indeed experiencing a great exhilaration. Yes, she was in the room with me but we were very far apart.

'Tirtha, after so many years!' She smiled and inhaled deeply.

'What were you doing with Tirtha behind closed doors?'

'What kind of a question is that? We were doing what everyone does.'

I did not know how surprised I should have felt by her answer.

'I don't understand what's happening.'

Nandini sprang up on the bed and answered my question with some short, incomprehensible bursts. 'My office! Tirtha—my boss! It's been only two months! Since his transfer from Delhi!'

'And then?'

'And then what do you think!' Nandini's eyes were shining. 'What could happen? I lost my mind when I saw him, Konkona! Absolutely. Lost. My. Mind. I can't tell you what came over me. I had forgotten all about him, but when I saw him after all these years, I realised I had just been going through the motions of life. I had nothing and no one to call my own. Still, I tried my best to hide my feelings from Tirtha. I spoke to him informally like I always had, I tried to be casual … but it didn't do me any good. One day, he grabbed my hand all of a sudden while dropping me home in his car and said, "Nandini, I want you back in my life." Konkona, what can I tell you? There was a tsunami in my heart! Believe me, I have always loved him but I never imagined that he was in love with me too.'

Red splotches spread across Nandini's fair face and her almond-brown eyes were ablaze with emotions. A thin stream of water cascaded down her cheeks. Nandini raised her voice and called out, 'Tirtha, listen!' There was no answer from Tirtha. I drew my knees close and shrank into my seat. I was caught in the crossfire of a new relationship between my old friends.

'Come on, let's see what he's up to!' Nandini said.

The two of us went into the study. Tirtha had covered his legs with a blanket and was deep in sleep. He appeared completely at home as he slept peacefully. Nandini ran her fingers through his hair.

'Hey, Tirtha! Get up,' she said suddenly tugging his hair. 'Konkona is here.'

Tirtha did not hear her.

'We spoke all night, Konkona. We booked the lower and middle berth but didn't sleep at all. We talked all the way. He told me how desperately he was in love with me, since he was seventeen or eighteen! I started to sob. I confessed my feelings and he started to cry too. Oh, we cried so much!' said Nandini. 'Let's sit in the other room. He won't wake up now.'

Nandini looked at Tirtha lovingly and without caring about my presence, pressed her lips wetly to his. She did not feel shy at all. As we walked out of the room, I thought to myself that, perhaps, at our age, it was indeed rather difficult to feel embarrassed.

It had started to rain. Jalapahar looked heavenly to me in the first rays of sunlight after a shower. I did not like the rain very much, it made me feel very blue.

I wanted to take a good look at Nandini. I hadn't seen her in a year. Debdutta, their son, she and I had gone to Park

Street for dinner. Puplu was a very sweet child. He was chubby with a ruddy complexion. I kept cuddling and caressing him.

'It's time you forgot Pushkar and settled down,' Nandini said when she saw the surge of affection I felt for her son.

Pushkar, my Pushkar! We were classmates at Kala Bhavan. Like a shanty washed away by a deluge, Pushkar and I had lost ourselves to the tides of love during the four years we were together. Then, for some reason, Pushkar disappeared from my life and I was still here, trying to stay afloat without him. These lonely mountains made me want to draw but I had only been able to create two or three paintings. I wanted a series of at least twelve paintings and call it 'Love and the Forest'. I was painting a couple in the forest for the project. But it was difficult to paint lovemaking scenes. The paintbrush always fell from my hand.

It was impossible to find similarities between the Nandini I met last year and the one who was sitting in front of me now. The old Nandini wore a big teep on her forehead, was draped in a blackish-green Mangalgiri saree, and had green glass bangles riding up her arms. However, this Nandini was an entirely new creature. Her quiet contentment had been replaced by a devil-may-care attitude. She was reckless and happy, and it was evident in how her lips curled and eyes shone. Tirtha and she had just had sex—her eyelashes told me as much and its intensity could be guessed from how ruffled her hair was.

'Please have lunch,' I said. 'I have told Shanta to make some for you.'

'Give Tirtha something to eat when he wakes up,' she said.

'That goes without saying.'

'Your mind is racing. Isn't it, Konkona?'

'Isn't that normal, Nandini? As far as I know, you were happy with Debdutta. You have a child together. This … all of a sudden?'

'I can't stand to be around Debdutta ever since Tirtha came back to my life. I hate being trapped with him.'

'And what about the child?'

'He's fine.'

'Where is he?'

'With my mother-in-law.'

'What did you say was your reason for coming here?'

'To meet you!'

'For how many days?'

'Not too many,' said Nandini and smiled. 'Three or four days. Deb and I have been fighting a lot recently. He probably thinks I've run away because I'm so angry with him. He didn't ask me too many questions. But my son kept calling out for me.'

'Nandini, are you being sensible?'

'Sensible about what? And what's the harm? All we've wanted is to be together, if only for a while. I was so thirsty, Konkona. Moreover, there's so much for us to talk about. He is married too and has two sons. I have a kid too. And yet, we can't imagine a single moment away from each other!'

'Are you serious about the relationship?'

'Of course, we are. Just talk to him. Talk to him when he wakes up—see what he says! He is not happy with his wife. They haven't had sex for the last two years.'

'Has he told you that?'

'I know it's true!' Nandini's eyes spilled over with tears. 'Why would he lie to me? You know, he calls me to his chamber twenty-five times a day just to have a look at me! Last night, on our way here, he did not take his eyes off me even for a minute. You won't believe how much he loves me.'

'We could've gone anywhere, stayed at a hotel but he's the regional manager,' Nandini continued after a pause for breath. 'He's the Head of the Eastern Division. We could run into a familiar face anywhere! Your place seemed the safest to me.'

Nandini was a sales executive of a well-known cell phone brand. Obviously, Tirtha was a higher-up in the same organisation.

'Okay, stay here. Talk among yourselves. But remember, Nandini, these things don't stay secret for long. Suppose Debdutta finds out you came here with Tirtha and I welcomed you knowing what you were up to and I abetted your extramarital affair. What will he think of me? Besides, this is a school. There are so many teachers and staff members here. What should I tell them about you two? What choice do I have but to introduce you as a married couple?'

'And aren't we like man and wife? Wake him up. Ask him if I'm not a wife to him!'

'You've lost your mind, Nandini. You know what you're doing is unacceptable.'

'Konkona, we'll live together very soon. He'll get out of his marriage and so will I. We'll live together. We love each other and we want each other. Who can stop us?'

'I don't know. I can't make any sense of this.'

'I have a terrible headache. Will you make me some coffee?'

Shanta was cleaning the kitchen. I told her not to knead the dough for dinner. We'd go out to eat. It was better for her to leave early. Shanta made three cups of coffee and served them in the bedroom.

'Let me wake him up,' said Nandini.

She went to wake Tirtha up. The sounds of her calling him drifted into my room. They were followed by sounds of playful admonitions and wet kisses. Then the door was slammed shut again without wasting any time. I sat frozen on my bed worrying about what Shanta might be thinking. Blood sloshed about in my veins with great ferocity. Two cups of coffee turned cold, waiting. I asked Shanta to leave at four-thirty and bolting the door shut, I quietly walked out of my home too. The strange sounds of flailing and flapping reached my ears. Was this what Nandini had meant by thirst?

I finished supper at six-thirty in the junior wing, completed preparations for the next day and headed home. I opened the door cautiously and was surprised to see Tirtha lying lazily on the drawing room couch and watching television. I could also hear the clamour of utensils in the kitchen. Nandini emerged into the drawing room as soon as she heard me open the door. Perhaps they had both showered and freshened up. Tirtha was in a kurta-pyjama and had a shawl wrapped around him and Nandini wore a pair of capris and a cardigan.

'Come, I've made coffee. It's so cold!' said Nandini.

Both of them looked extremely content. It felt like this was their home and I had dropped in for a cup of coffee.

'Konkona, how many years has it been?' Tirtha chimed in.

'I didn't think I'd see you again,' I said sitting in a chair at a distance from them.

'You're quite surprised, aren't you?' Tirtha asked pompously.

No one would say he was my guest and not the other way round. I suppose he had forgotten it too. He remained seated with his legs flung one over the other. A lit cigarette drooped from his fingers. He may have been talking to me, but his eyes were glued to the TV.

'So? How's it going?'

'Fine.'

'Not much headway with your paintings. Is that why you ran away to the hills?' he asked.

'A splendid conclusion!' I answered with a laugh.

'Am I wrong? What rubbish are you teaching the kids to draw? A vase with flowers?' Tirtha scratched his cheek.

A peculiar masculine fire bubbled within him. I remembered how skinny he used to be as a boy. He never joined the boys in their games and preferred to play tag and other simple games with us girls instead. But, Tirtha was no longer that young boy. At thirty-three or thirty-four, he was quite handsome and very successful. Nandini was pretty even as a child. The rigours of domesticity had briefly tamed her beauty, but the affair with Tirtha had pumped life back into her.

Nandini brought three cups of coffee and put the tray on the centre table. She snuggled against Tirtha on the couch. He pulled her to his chest as if on cue and Nandini rested her head on his shoulder.

'We'll go out for dinner tonight,' I said turning my eyes away. 'At seven-thirty.'

'Absolutely not!' Nandini exclaimed in a coquettish, nasal voice.

'What do you mean? There's no food at home.'

'Tch, forget it. We'll have toast and butter,' Tirtha answered, his voice dripping with annoyance. 'And an omelette. That'll do.'

'I'm quite hungry,' said Nandini. She pouted like a child and said something unintelligibly.

'Hungry? Oh? Are you now?' Tirtha whispered to her.

I got up and left the room seeing them flirt with each other. I decided to take a shower and change my clothes. I briefly wondered if I should go to the shops and buy some pasta, cheese and eggs. Some paneer and chicken too. What would they eat if I were to host them for the next three days? Then I changed my mind. They were starving but it was a different kind of hunger. I could treat them like my guests but they were not really interested in my hospitality. In fact, they were not even affected by my presence. All they needed was a safe space, a place where they could be together. My three-foot-wide bed had become their island.

Someone had to make the toasts and omelettes. I put on a warm housecoat and went into the kitchen at eight o'clock. Tirtha and Nandini were in the study and the door was ajar. I could hear raised voices, edgy exchanges. I could make out that they were discussing something complicated. Nandini raised her voice even higher. She wanted Tirtha to come clean to his wife right away. She was ready to disclose the relationship to her husband, too, and walk out of her home. Tirtha tried to reason with her that such haste would not do them good.

'Tirtha, we've been away from each other for so long. I'll die if I can't be with you now!' Nandini wailed.

'I'm yours, Nandini. I am yours alone. There's no one else.'

'Lies! All lies! Only your wife can lay claim to you! What right do I have? Didn't I see how you were dancing with Tikli at Mohit's party? I couldn't stand it, Tirtha! All the time she was there, you either had your arm around her waist or her shoulders. I don't believe that you two don't have sex anymore. Swear on Monty that you don't sleep with her.'

'No, Nandini. That's not right. I can't swear on my own child. Have I ever asked you if you sleep with Debdutta?'

'You know fully well that I don't. I have put a stop to everything. I have refused him each time since I met you. You know how much shit I have to face because of this. Tirtha, I'm going through hell!'

'You have to accept him, Nandini. He's your husband, after all.'

'No, he's no one to me. I love you. I'll hang myself if you tell me to. Just please don't mess with me.'

'Nandini, I've told you many times that my marriage with Tikli is not unhappy like yours and Debdutta's.'

'Oh, Tirtha! Shut up! Shut up, please. Leave me alone. Don't you feel bad going on and on about your wife in front of me?'

'Come here, Nandini. Come.'

I assumed that after this Nandini buried her face in Tirtha's chest. I spotted a packet of corn in the refrigerator. Corn toast for dinner sounded rather nice. I was about to take it out of the fridge when the phone started to ring. It was Tirtha's or Nandini's cell phone.

'Please answer. It's Debdutta,' said Nandini running into the kitchen with her phone.

'Why should I?' I asked, taken aback.

'I can't talk to him now. He'll ask me all sorts of questions. I had a fight with him before coming here so I can give him the cold shoulder. I don't want to talk to him.'

'What should I say to him?'

'You can say something. Say that I'm very upset. I've worked myself up into a state and I'm sleeping it off.'

'Nandini, I can't. So many lies …'

'Please, please, I beg you. Just repeat whatever I told you. Otherwise, he won't stop calling!'

'This is called adultery, by the way.'

'Are you jealous, Konkona?'

'Jealous?'

'That's what I think.'

'Oh dear! I pity you.'

'Hello,' I said after snatching the phone from her hands.

'Konkona?'

It was Debdutta on the other side. He was in deep distress and it was evident in his voice. I could hear regret too.

'Hi. Um, Nandini is sleeping, that's why I answered the call.'

'Thank God, she's with you. Thank God! What foolishness is she up to, Konkona? We had a fight and she ran away to the mountains! God knows what she might end up doing. I can't tell you how worried I was. Thank God, she turned up at your place!'

'Don't worry, I'll take care of her …'

'Is she asleep?'

'Yes.'

'How do you think she is?'

'She went to bed as soon as she arrived here. We didn't get to speak.'

'Could you please remove the sleeping pills from her handbag?'

'Alright.'

'I don't know what's got into her. She quarrels with me without any reason, picks fights, doesn't even spare a glance for Puplu. She was not like this. Konkona, will you please try to find out what's going on with her? Maybe it's something at work. And if it is, just tell her to quit her job. I can take care of everything. We can do without a second income.'

'I'll have a word with her.'

'I'm very worried about Puplu. I couldn't control my temper yesterday. I shouted at her and in response, she slammed a vase against the wall. And after that, she ran out of the house. I think Puplu has run up a fever because of us. I'm taking him to the doctor now.'

Debdutta hung up. Nandini's eyes bore a crazed look.

'What did he say?'

'Puplu has a fever. Because the two of you fought. Or maybe because you're not with him.'

'Yes, it's been an entire day.'

Nandini went back to the study.

Tirtha's phone rang as we were sitting down to eat.

'Hello?' he said brusquely as though he was in a critical meeting and the phone had gone off rudely when it wasn't supposed to. His self-confidence was astounding—no one could suspect him for a moment. Especially his wife who was many miles away from him. Nandini looked at him sharply. Tirtha put a finger to his lips, ordering us to be quiet.

'Yes, Tikli. I'm having dinner. No, no, I'm not drinking! Absolutely alright. I'll go to bed now and sleep.

'Monty? Monty? Hi, Baba. I'm here. Won't you sleep? Yes, yes, I'll come to get your report card. Your Ma will too. Give me a goodnight kiss!

'Yes, Tikli, you go to bed too. I will, I will. Okay, bye. Goodnight!'

Fat tears rolled down Nandini's cheeks. Tirtha hung up and looked at her impassively for a few moments.

'Nandini,' he said finally.

'You, Tirtha … you …! You have a completely normal relationship with your wife. Then, why are you with me?'

'How many times will I have to answer this question, Nandini?'

'As many times as I want. You're taking me for a ride. Her too! This can't go on. No! You have to make a choice.'

Anger rose in Tirtha's blood as he pushed away the chair and rose from the table. He washed his hands and went into the study. Nandini did not leave her seat but she could not stop crying either. I got up and started putting the plates away.

I was woken from sleep sometime around midnight. Nandini's voice. I sat up in my bed. What was going on? Why was she crying? Or was she howling? I tried to figure out what was happening. It took me no more than a few seconds. Tirtha was devouring her. A tempest was blowing through the other room and Nandini was moaning from the pains and pleasures of lovemaking. Screaming! I could hear Tirtha's frantic whispers.

'Let me go, Tirtha! Let me go! I'll die, oh!' said Nandini. The house was swinging, swinging madly.

The next morning, before leaving for work, I wanted to push open the door to the study to see the ruins from the previous night. I found Nandini asleep on Tirtha's chest. He was deep in sleep with his mouth wide open. They snored gently together. The crumpled sheet revealed the contours of their unclothed bodies. Seeing them entangled this way was like looking into a world where there was no suffering or heartache. No shame or guilt. They had come to an understanding and formed a plan. Nandini would walk out on her husband, son and mother-in-law, and Tirtha would abandon his marriage and child. They'd rent a place and live together. A legal separation from their respective spouses would soon follow. As straightforward an arrangement as any.

This time, I called the number without any forethought.

'Konkona, is she okay?' Debdutta sounded terribly vulnerable.

'She is fine but she does not want to speak with you. I'm on my way to school.'

'I understand. All I want is for her to be alright. There's nothing left to say anyway. I will leave her alone. Let her do whatever she wants to. I have no right to stop her from doing what she pleases. Let her come home in the dead of the night or not at all! But this boy, he just won't stop crying. Tell her that she'll pay for her sins. The passage of time is just as selfish as she is. She'll find out soon enough what being so self-centred does to a woman—'

'Let it be, Debdutta. I don't want to listen to any of this.'

'Can you tell me when she plans to come back?'

I told Nandini her husband wanted to know when she would be home again.

'I don't know!' Nandini bit her lips and shouted in response.

Debdutta hung up. He had heard her clearly from the other side.

'Why aren't you speaking to your husband?' Tirtha, who was standing behind Nandini wanted to know.

'What do you mean? Why do you want me to do that?' Nandini turned around to face Tirtha and asked.

'Have you ever stopped to think about him?'

What had appeared to be harmless questions asked in the dark of the night had planted deep suspicions in the daylight. Every small misunderstanding brought forth a deluge of questions. This was to be expected in relationships such as theirs.

'I have met Debdutta twice, Konkona,' Tirtha said to me. 'He might be ill-tempered but he's very much in love with Nandini.'

'So what?' Nandini was frothing at the mouth. 'What can I do about it? Should I let him fuck me? After all, this man will not leave his wife. He'll paw at her at the first call of hunger. Isn't that right? And I have to fuck my husband and him too!'

Tirtha lit a cigarette. The tenderness and pleasure from last night were disappearing swiftly like dandelion bristles blowing in the wind.

'What's the big deal? It's nothing new. You'll have to keep a distance, that's all.'

'What a man you are, Tirtha.'

'Don't be so dramatic, Nandini. I haven't suggested anything unreasonable.'

'I know. I know you keep your wife nicely satisfied. That's why you are asking the same from me.'

'Well, that's my duty.'

I listened to them standing in my spot. Perhaps Shanta was eavesdropping too.

'Then why did you lie to me? Why did you say you haven't fucked your wife ever since she had the child?'

'We don't really. A monotony has set in …'

'Asshole! Why are you fucking with me?' Nandini lunged at Tirtha.

'When did I do that? Am I not on vacation with you? Am I not trying to show you a good time?'

'I gave you everything, Tirtha.'

'And haven't I, Nandini?'

Nandini slapped Tirtha squarely on the cheek.

'Do you take me for a fool?' she asked.

'You've lost your mind. Just because you're sleeping with your lover in the twenty-first century doesn't mean you'll accuse him of whatever you feel like! Would you have an affair with me if you weren't getting anything in return?'

'What did I have to get from you, Tirtha? You're the one who started this. We've been friends for so long. I've loved you ever since I was little. How could I refuse you? Could I ever turn you down?'

'Of course you had something to gain from this, Nandini! Don't forget the twenty-two-lakh-rupee loan I arranged for you.'

'I didn't accept it, did I, Tirtha?' Nandini was crying like a woman possessed.

'That's because you decided to leave your family.'

'I was wrong, wasn't I? I shouldn't have loved you so much and trusted you so blindly.'

'Loving someone can never be wrong.'

'It's bullshit, total bullshit!' Nandini threw herself on the couch.

A touch of sympathy shone in Tirtha's eyes. He rubbed out the cigarette into the ashtray and held Nandini from behind.

'Leave everything to me. I'll take care of it. Have patience. Things will take their course. But you are hell-bent on separating me from my family. You wouldn't be so selfish if you loved me truly.'

'I'm selfish, is that so? I'll put an end to my marriage, give up everything just to be with you and you'll go on with your family like everything is normal? You've never spared me a thought.'

'No matter how hard you try to be modern, wear jeans and skirts, the truth is you and all of you are victims of a herd mentality.'

My phone started to ring. It was my mother.

'Hello, Ma,' I said. The two of them had quietened down.

'Shanta told me you have visitors. Who is it? You didn't tell me anything.'

'Oh, yes. Nandini.'

'With the child?'

'No.'

I hung up soon after. I had a class coming up and it was time for me to leave.

'I have a headache,' said Tirtha. 'Tell the girl to make me a cup of coffee.'

I gave Shanta instructions.

'How long will this vacation last?' I asked Tirtha.

'At first, I'd thought of four or five days. But I don't know. I'm under a lot of pressure. You can see it's no longer a vacation.'

I felt greatly anxious about how long I would have to tolerate this under my roof.

'I have a suggestion, Tirtha.' I blurted out. 'Instead of wasting time fighting with each other why don't the two of you talk it out like adults? It's time you made a decision. This is not a casual affair, so what's the point of suffering day after day? Moreover, you two are friends and have been friends for many years. It's not something to slip in and out of casually.' I started to feel sentimental all of a sudden.

'If she has fallen in love with you so deeply then it's unfair to expect her to go back to Debdutta and pretend that everything is fine. She can leave her marriage if she wants to and take the child along with her. She's financially independent. She just needs your little support in this fight.'

'Support?'

'For example, you could find a place for her. Provide some financial help in the beginning. A good lawyer to expedite the divorce. She needs someone by her side.'

'Are you trying to make a deal with me, Konkona?' Tirtha narrowed his eyes.

'Deal?' I was so surprised that the shawl slipped off my shoulders in response. 'What do you mean?'

'Have you two ganged up to put pressure on me?'

By the time I understood what he was implying, there was nothing left for me to say. The humiliation I felt was sharp and strong. I looked at Nandini.

'Nandini?' I asked.

She did not feel slighted like me. Instead, her face had contorted into ugly lines.

'Who told you to speak on my behalf?' she spat at me. 'Am I a fucking beggar that I need his support? And who are you to tell him how he should support me? He'll help me depending on what I need. Do you understand? I know you're jealous of me. You don't want good things to happen to me. You are jealous.'

I looked at Tirtha.

'Tirtha, how do you think I would've benefited from this *deal*?' I asked. 'You're good at negotiations, you handle a company's business—so tell me.'

I was about to leave when I noticed an empty bottle of whisky under the kitchen sink. Tirtha had drunk in my study despite my strict instructions not to.

'No one can predict the ending of an illegitimate relationship,' I said without looking at them. Some people even kill or get killed. Don't do any such thing in my home. Please.'

Nandini burst into tears again.

The boys sat down for prep after supper. A wispy but unshakeable night descended on the mountains. It was very cold. I went to see Alomita instead of going home. She asked me about my guests and I told her about them. She asked me more questions, I answered all of them truthfully.

'You still haven't thrown them out, Konkona?' Alomita was furious. 'I'll do it if you don't. They're total frauds; they don't even pretend to be decent people. How are you tolerating this? And why?'

'Because I know they'll leave when the time is right,' I said. 'I want to see how long this will go on.'

The flat was dark when I returned at eight o'clock. The door to the studio was shut. A sliver of light streamed through the narrow slit under the door. I did not need to eavesdrop.

I could hear the rough sounds of their lovemaking, their conversation—there was no static.

'Promise me, give me your word, you won't leave me.'

Tirtha seemed to have undergone severe physical exertion.

'No, I won't go away. I promise,' he answered, catching his breath.

'Promise me you'll love me like this till your dying breath.'

'Not just your body,' he moaned. 'I'm crazy for you.'

'Tirtha, will we ever live together?'

'Oh, yes! Just … give me … some time.'

It looked like they had come to an understanding.

I went to the kitchen to arrange dinner.

I didn't notice it at first but Tirtha's phone kept ringing continuously from nine-thirty. He was either speaking in low tones on the freezing balcony or trying to stay out of earshot in the dining room. Nandini had drunk a lot in the study. Tirtha was intoxicated too, but he was trying his best to sound coherent while speaking on the phone.

I was about retreat into my room after asking them to have dinner. However, all of a sudden, Nandini came running to me in a dishevelled state. She did not appear to be in the right state of mind.

'See! Just see the messages Tikli has been sending to Tirtha.'

Tirtha came running. He tried to snatch the phone from Nandini's hands.

'Don't you think about me even once all day?' Nandini was reading the text messages loudly. She was screaming.

I covered my ears.

'This is a school, Nandini! Have both of you forgotten?'

Nandini was beating her breast.

'Oh, oh! Just listen to what Tirtha has done. He's taken the fortnight off from work. He'll be with me for three days and after that he's jetting off to Malaysia with his wife and kid! The tickets are booked. He brought me here on the train, refused to stay at a hotel so that he could fuck me for two days. He'll suck me dry and leave me to the dogs before he rushes off to please his wife. His wife will strut around the beach in a bikini while he shoots her on a Handycam. Tirtha, why did you make a fool of me? All this time? I'll call Tikli right away and tell her everything.'

I was numb with fear. Meanwhile, the two of them had started clawing each other in an attempt to wrest control of the phone. In an entirely unexpected move, Tirtha struck a blow on Nandini's face. She fell over but did not let go of him.

'I have nothing left, Tirtha. My home, my husband, my baby—I left everything to be with you. Where will I go now? Tell me. Why did you have to ruin my life? Why?' She grabbed his legs and beseeched.

'I'll not let you off so easily,' she seethed. 'I will tell Tikli everything. I'll make sure to ruin your life. I promise you.'

Tirtha kicked Nandini off him and stormed into the study. Nandini, half-naked and severely distressed, crumpled to the floor and started crying.

'Where will I go now? How will I show my face?' The cries grew louder and more garbled.

I can't say when I fell asleep. Small sounds in the dead of the night woke me up. The door to my bedroom was open. Nandini was missing from my room. The drawing room light was on. It wasn't night any longer. The phone showed that it was five in the morning. The sun was usually out at this hour but today, it was still dark. Perhaps the clouds were still looming in the sky. I woke up without making a sound and made my way to the study. Nandini was asleep on her stomach while Tirtha was quietly packing his bags. So, Nandini had spent the night with Tirtha even after everything that happened.

Tirtha was surprised to see me. He paused for a moment. 'Konkona, it's time for me to leave.'

'Right now?'

'Yes. Tikli is getting suspicious. She's been calling me nonstop and sending me weird texts. Plus, Nandini is not safe anymore. Who can say what she'll end up doing?'

'Will she stay here?'

'Take care of her, please. You can do it. And tell her if Tikli gets to know about us, then either she'll be fired from her job or I will. She shouldn't try to reach out to Tikli, no matter what happens. Also, she hasn't lost anything! Debdutta, the cuckold, will take her back.'

'Won't you say goodbye to her?'

'Are you mad?'

Tirtha left before it was five-thirty. He didn't even spare a final glance at Nandini. I lay down on my bed again. I was not in the mood to go out. God knew how Nandini would react when she woke up. I did not want her to do anything reckless. I got hold of her purse and threw away the sleeping pills just like Debdutta had told me to.

Nandini had drunk a lot last night. It was eleven o'clock when she woke up. I was sitting quietly at my study table.

'Where's he?' Nandini asked, blinking frantically when she saw I was alone.

'Gone. Early morning.'

No sound escaped from Nandini. She buried her face in her hands and stayed that way for a while.

'Has he taken all his things?' she asked after a few moments.

'Yes. He's warned you not to bother Tikli if you care about your job.'

Nandini stared at me blankly.

'I'll quit this job, I think. My phone is out of power. Will you give me yours? I want to talk to Puplu.'

I fetched my phone from the other room. She reached for it with both hands.

'I've made a mess of your room,' she added. 'Don't worry, I'll clean it before I leave.'

THE BEDROOM

Time had come to a standstill for Anandi. On any other day, she would have had no problem sitting idle. The fact that she was waiting would become obvious if she sat still—so she went from room to room arranging and re-arranging things. She even made a quick trip to the terrace. The Ganga flowed right next to the house. On other days, she did not think twice before going to the riverside to sit on the benches or the steps leading into the water. This was not possible today—she would draw attention and that would not be desirable. The kitchen had been busy since morning in anticipation of the guests—there could be no oversight in planning, enthusiasm or love.

Chhotopishi, her youngest aunt, had already arrived with her husband the previous day. Just like her mother had wanted.

Her mother's older brother and his wife, Boromama and Boromami, arrived in the morning. Pupu was delirious with joy in the company of his grand uncles and grand aunts. The older members of the family were pleasantly surprised by his incessant prattle. The house was bursting with laughter at the six-year-old boy's antics. There was happiness in the air; still, no one was as happy as Anandi. She hadn't seen her mother smile in the last two years—she was always ready to leak tears, sometimes without any rhyme or reason. But today, her eyes shone with sheer joy. She was drenched in sweat but discomfort mattered little to her—everything must be shipshape, she had to ensure it. Her mother could not stop looking at Anandi. Maybe she was trying to gauge the motions of her heart. Her mother had made a small blunder when she came into Anandi's room to wake her up in the morning.

'Should I remove Sutanu and your photo from the drawing room and keep it in my room? Or yours?' she said, stroking Anandi's head,

Anandi was not exactly the rebellious kind. She had never felt the need to protest strongly against anything. Moreover, no major decision had been forced upon her without approval. If she ever had to go against her wishes and agree to something she did not want, the most she would do was cry. And then, someone would reason with her and she would almost always concede. Conversely, her crying and general displeasure were enough to make a person retreat and relieve her of stress. This morning, as was her nature, she burst into tears upon hearing her mother's proposal. As was her mother's nature too, she was startled by Anandi's tears. The talks were already in progress, so much had already happened. Suppose Anandi changed her mind now, and backed out just because she felt like it! What would happen then! Her mother did not realise that Anandi did not really mind removing the photo of a happy couple on their wedding anniversary from the drawing room.

She had adequately grieved Sutanu's death and cried copiously but the tears on this occasion did not bear a similar grief. She was crying because Sutanu—missing, dead—would be forced to fade into nothingness yet again. The day when

Sutanu would no longer exist in her life, even as a photograph, was fast approaching. Anandi could do little but accept it. But not before shedding a few tears for him. She was a simple, uncomplicated woman and she was fully aware that it was not possible to start over with a new man while still mourning her dead husband.

'But tell me, will you ever forget Sutanu?' Kaberi, her childhood friend, had asked her.

'It is impossible to forget anything, Kaberi. Those who claim to do so are nothing but liars. What matters is how we remember the person. I don't want to mourn Sutanu in a way that'll put my life on hold. I married Sutanu, he is Pupu's father, we were married for less than six years. Still, I'll never forget him or what he liked to talk about, his dreams, his love for me—I can never forget it,' replied Anandi, quite surprised.

'Some other man taking Sutanu's place. Don't you have doubts? Don't you feel hurt?'

'I'm feeling everything except these two!' Anandi had answered.

'What should I do with the photo then?' her mother asked seeing her cry. 'I'll do whatever you tell me to. I could keep it in the drawing room but it will catch everyone's attention.'

A little later, Anandi removed the photo and hung it above her bedroom door.

Her father and various aunts and uncles were chatting in the long verandah enclosed by bamboo blinds. Her mother was in the kitchen while her Chhotopishi had gone for a shower. Today's discussion, led by her father, was about the house. It started with his father making the fateful journey to Chandannagar and his refusal to indulge in double-dealing or any sort of fraudulent activities while he built his small business during the tumultuous period of the Second World War. Then, the house was constructed, which, in the beginning, was nothing more than a few rooms. With time, the rooms were made bigger and new ones were added. Her father was proud of the house and its history but the regret in his voice was unmissable. He still felt guilty about not being able to take his father's business to great heights despite inheriting all of it. Anandi came to the verandah looking for Pupu.

'Finish your shower, Khuku,' said her aunt, 'Take some rest after lunch. You can get ready later.'

'I'm looking for Pupu. I'll go for a bath once he's done with his.'

'Komola has given Pupu his bath. She's feeding him now,' said her mother.

'Why don't I know this?' Anandi was used to bathing and feeding Pupu every day and wondered why her mother asked Komola to step in today.

'Getting Pupu to eat is a two-hour-long battle. He'll run off to the terrace or the garden and he'll make all of us chase him. You won't be able to feed him today and get ready on time. It'll be two o'clock before you know it. What about your shower, lunch? That's why I asked Komola ...'

Her mother turned to look at her older brother's wife, seeking reassurance.

'Well done! Send Pupu to take a nap,' Boromami chimed in.

'It's important that they meet our Pupubabu, isn't it?' her uncle asked. 'Don't let him sleep through it all.'

'Oh, God! If we don't pack him off to bed now, he'll become extremely cranky in the evening and drive us up the wall!' her father exclaimed. 'If there's a power cut, he'll spend the entire evening at the riverside and refuse to come home. But if the little devil goes off to sleep in the afternoon, he'll be in a good mood later. Tuck him to bed right now!'

'Oh, is that so? Does the power often go out in the evening? Abani, have you made arrangements in that case? Candles, et cetera?'

'Yes, yes, everything is taken care of, Dada. Still, I pray to God that the lights stay on today. Isn't it very hot too?' said her mother.

Anandi went into her room. She had nothing else to do. It was really very hot and she could do with a shower. Feeling shy, she decided to wait for her mother to hurry her up. She was used to taking a postprandial siesta and often fell asleep as she tried to get Pupu to nap. She could still sneak in a nap if only she had had her lunch already. They were supposed to arrive no later than half past three.

She wasn't aware that she was standing in front of the mirror when Chhotopishi's voice pulled her out of her reverie.

'Wait a minute, I have something to say to you,' she said to Anandi as she dried her wet hair with a towel. 'What saree will you wear in the evening?' She continued as she applied vermilion in the parting of her hair.

Anandi had a feeling Chhotopishi was doing her mother's bidding on her behalf. She hadn't dared ask Anandi this question herself.

'Tell me which saree I should wear,' said Anandi.

'Open your almirah. I'll pick something.'

Anandi did what Chhotopishi asked her to. It was a massive wooden cupboard from a bygone era. There were mirrors fitted on both doors. The sarees were arranged in stacks and there were a few salwar suit sets too. Would anyone believe that Anandi hadn't already picked out a saree? She had her eyes set on a bottle-green tissue saree with a narrow zari border and covered with zari dots. It was very delicate and elegant. And so light that she often forgot she was wearing it at all!

'What do you think of this one?' she asked her Chhotopishi.

'Not such a dark colour, and definitely not such a fine one! Your skin will show,' said her aunt vehemently.

'This is perfect. You can do without jewellery too,' she said after settling on a saffron saree with a pink border. She offered her advice and left the room.

Standing under the shower, Anandi could not stop the tears from streaming down her cheeks. These were not tears of objection or accusation. She was reminded of the day eight years ago when Sutanu's family had come to see her for the first time. They had made her wear a bright red muslin saree and gold jewellery. Today, too, she would be presented to the groom's family with great expectations, but unlike last time, she had been advised to wear a subdued, simple saree. Chhotopishi had warned her against showing skin. Muslin sarees were rarely modest, yet that had not been a problem the last time.

The truth was, the status of the girl who was meeting the groom today had changed. Arrangements were being made for her second marriage, but the fact that she was a widow could not be forgotten. In fact, her new in-laws would not be pleased if her widow status bore no mark on her appearance or how she dressed. They would be forced to assume that the would-be bride had little regard for the sanctity of marriage. It was true she had lost her husband at a very young age and it made little sense for her to be alone for the rest of her days. Was it fair for her to perish slowly from loneliness? No, none of them wanted that. However, it also did not mean she would march to the wedding altar grinning and gleaming like a first-time bride. Instead, she would have to walk on tiptoes and let her uneasiness be known to everyone present. Or else, everyone would think her vulgar. If she had to impress the groom's family today, then it wouldn't bode well to adorn herself with heavy jewellery and a gaudy saree. She had to dress today, not as someone celebrating a festival but as a spectator watching it from afar.

The story of the groom's family was rather interesting. The groom, Bitan Sinha Roy, was a distant relative of Chhotopishi's in-laws. Bitan had met Anandi for the first time at her cousin's wedding last winter. He had liked her right away and did not object to Pupu or her past. He sent a proposal through Chhotopishi, and Anandi's parents were over the moon about it. They had secretly wanted Anandi to marry again but they never thought the groom would turn up from within their circle. Her mother had burst into tears of joy on the day Bitan Sinha Roy had spoken to them for the first time on the phone.

'I give you my thousand blessings, Bitan. You're a very kind-hearted person,' she said.

Bitan and his family were not coming today to assess Anandi's candidature for a wife but to finalise the union.

'Your son won't go to sleep unless you are there. Go lie down with him for a bit,' her mother said as she emerged from the bathroom 'One shouldn't go to bed on an empty stomach after taking a shower,' she added and stuffed a sweet into Anandi's mouth.

'Come here, Ma. Come,' said Pupu excitedly, thumping the bed when he saw her. She shut the door behind her and lay down next to her son.

'Ma, you're so cold,' Pupu said hugging his mother tightly.

'No more talking. Sleep now. And remember, in the evening, don't be a naughty boy in front of the visitors. If you are asked to leave the room for a while, please go with Komola-di. Alright? Don't say, "No, I won't." Don't be stubborn.'

'Will we go to their house today?'

'Whose house?'

'The visitors.'

'And who told you so?' Anandi laughed.

Pupu could not remember who it was. It was everyone who had told him of such a possibility.

'Not today. But today we'll decide when.'

'Dadu and Dida won't go, will they? Only you and I. Won't Dadu and Dida cry then? Won't it make them sad?'

'Not too much. Otherwise, would they let us go?'

'But why do we have to go away?' Pupu slipped his hand into his mother's blouse.

'Dadu and Dida are getting old. Who will look after us?'

'You'll marry someone, won't you, Ma?'

'Yes.'

'And what if he also dies like Baba?'

'Does everyone drop dead that easily?'

Pupu blew raspberries and fell asleep soon after. Anandi propped him against a bolster and settled him in comfortably. Next, she got hold of her cotton saree, laid it out on the bed, put the pleats in place with pins, and got it ready to wear later in the day. It was a new saree and she still struggled to manage it. Komola-di called her for lunch. She had just finished eating and had gone into her room when Bitan arrived with his entire troupe. Chhotopishi came running into her room.

'Apply only a little bit of lipstick. They won't be able to take their eyes off you,' she advised her.

How the times had changed. When Sutanu and his family had come to see her, she had to sit quietly with her head lowered. It was partly out of shyness and partly her mother's instructions. But today, as soon as she stepped into the living room, Bitan stood up.

'Welcome, welcome. I was looking for you,' he said. 'Where's the little one?'

'Asleep!' she answered with a smile. She was not a young girl after all. What did she have to be shy about?

'Your aunt had a great time with him at Payel's wedding!' Chhotopishi said with a smile.

'Pupu can't stand moustaches. "My father didn't have one, nor does my Dadu. You should chop yours off too!" he had said to me. Haven't you noticed, Anandi? I've shaved it off.'

She was taken by surprise. She exhaled quietly.

'Yes, I have,' she answered.

Bitan was accompanied by one of his sisters and her husband. His mother couldn't come. Her rheumatism had got worse and she hadn't been able to get up from bed for the last few days. She had written a letter to Anandi's father saying she had agreed to the marriage. She had also requested that Chhotopishemoshai and Bitan's sister fix a date and time for the wedding. She had sent her love to Anandi and Pupu.

Bitan had always been like this. He loved to live it up. Everyone was quick to laugh at his jokes but he always stayed within limits and never overdid it. He had a very distinct personality. The families got talking and the tea and snacks were served. The evening had just set in when Pupu woke up and he was delighted to see Bitan. Anandi's father gave Bitan and his family a tour of their beloved house. The tales of the house were recounted again. She noticed that Bitan had not let go of Pupu's hand. The sight made her very happy. The lights went off a little later like they did every evening.

'Shall we go to the riverside?' Bitan said.

'Let the two of them go. They might have something to say to each other,' Sulekha, Bitan's sister-in-law, said.

All of them agreed in unison. Pupu was not with the group at that time. Anandi and Bitan walked through the garden and arrived at the river. It was the family's private ghat and so there were no strangers lurking around. The water of the Ganga shone under the lights. The river flowed by. Bitan sat close to Anandi.

'This is so beautiful!' he said.

A siren went off in one of the factories. The workday had come to an end.

'When I got married to Sutanu, the thing I was most sad to leave behind in this house was the river, the fact that I couldn't sit by it whenever I wanted to,' Anandi said. 'Once we were done with our lessons, my friends and I would come here and chat till late into the night. We sang songs. Not every house had a TV then.'

'And now? Don't you hang out here till late into the night anymore?'

'Where are my friends?' she said laughing. 'All of them have left. I did too, but I had to come back.'

'I was told that there aren't many people in your husband's family. But who's still around?' Bitan asked.

'My father-in-law and Sutanu's sister. My father-in-law lives with his daughter. I left for Rourkela right after the wedding. That's why I never really got the chance to know my in-laws very well.'

'But shouldn't you let them know either way?'

'I suppose my parents will.'

'Will they protest?'

'I don't think so.'

'Will they ask for Pupu?'

'No, no. They would never!' she replied, widening her eyes.

'Alright then.'

'Look, Anandi, a lot of people are saying that my decision to marry you is a display of my kindness,' said Bitan after a few moments of silence. 'Just the other day, my mother called me and said, "Bitan, kindness is meant for strangers, don't bring someone into your home just because you pity them. You're marrying Anandi because you like her, you want to spend all your life together. If this isn't true, then you shouldn't go ahead with the marriage." Ma is absolutely right. When I saw you for the first time at Payel's wedding, you were wearing a blue saree, remember? … I did not know who you were but the fact that I'm here sitting with you is because of the intense attraction I had felt for you then. I still feel the same affection for you. I have no ulterior motives.'

'But tell me one thing, Bitan. You saw me, you liked me, you started to like me so much that soon enough you were thinking about marrying me,' Anandi replied. 'Then you heard Pupu call me Ma. You asked around and found out about my past. But by now, you had become stubborn in your affection for me, my past was just an aside. But if we were to imagine that you had never seen a woman and she had a past just like me, and her family had sent a proposal to you, in that case, would you even consider it?'

'I don't know what you're looking for, Anandi. In any case, I don't have an answer for you. I was so busy trying to get the business to take off that I had no time to think about marriage. I was in a relationship with a distant cousin when I was much younger and no one since then. But all I knew was that if I were to marry, I'd do it for love. And that's what I am doing now.'

The lights came back on while the two were still talking.

'Are you still in touch with your cousin?' Anandi asked Bitan.

'No, no! She married years ago and lives abroad,' Bitan said, laughing heartily.

'I'm against the idea of hiring a band, feeding the entire clan and chanting religious mantras to get married,' Bitan added as they rose to go home. 'What about you, Anandi?'

'I don't want a big wedding either', she said.

A day towards the end of the month of Baisakh was fixed for Anandi's wedding to Bitan. It was not a big wedding, true, but because Anandi's parents and Bitan's mother wanted it, they arranged for a priest who got them married in a traditional Hindu ceremony. On the night before the wedding, because she was soft-hearted, she found herself sobbing holding Sutanu's photograph. In fact, she was sobbing so much and feeling so sad that at one point, she felt she was being unfair to Sutanu. She should not have let go of Sutanu without at least putting up a fight. There was a time when he meant everything to her.

But now that he was dead, did he no longer mean anything to her? Did she not even feel the need to honour his memory? Sutanu had devoted his life to her. Their conjugal life resurfaced in Anandi's mind. She remembered all the ways Sutanu ensured she lived happily. She was not in love with Bitan. It would have been a matter of some consolation if she were. Was she so desperate that she agreed to the first proposal that came her way? A relationship of so many years, a happy marriage, Pupu—were these not enough to live a full life? Just like her, Sutanu was also severed from his fairytale existence, wasn't he? Why couldn't she think of a life where it was just her and Pupu? Why was she so weak?

In the dark of the night, she put her hands on a sleeping Pupu's cheeks. Something sticky grazed her fingers. Taken by surprise, she turned on the bedside switch and the room flooded with light. Her fingers were bloody and so were Pupu's cheeks. Blood? Where did it come from? It took only a few seconds for Anandi to lose her mind upon seeing blood. As far as she was concerned, it was Sutanu's restless soul that had inflicted harm on their child. What else could it be, of course, this was the only explanation. Soon after she realised it was a mosquito's doing. It had swollen up after sucking the child's blood. Unable to fly, it was stuck to his skin and had finally succumbed between Anandi's fingers. She sighed deeply and got off the bed.

'The wedding's tomorrow. No point thinking about all this now,' she said to herself while washing her hands.

The next day, as she was preparing to leave for her marital home, uncertainty stirred in the hearts of her relatives. Anandi had refused to dress up in wedding finery like a young bride to go to her in-laws. The reason being that she wanted Pupu to travel in the same car as her. Holding her six-year-old son's hand while being dressed up in a bride's colours, wearing a wedding tiara would be a rather odd sight.

'You should be on your way,' they protested. 'Chhotopishi will drop Pupu an hour or so later. All rituals will be done by then. If you don't mind, we could give him a shower, feed him lunch, make him take a nap and drop him off in the evening. Their house will be full of people. Who will bathe him, run after him while he refuses to eat in the middle of chaos? You're a new bride and won't be able to chase him around the house in front of Bitan's relatives.'

This was enough to make Anandi start crying out of fear. She exclaimed that she wouldn't leave unless Pupu came along with her. She wouldn't go anywhere.

'Are you already separating the two of us? she said.

'I won't go anywhere without Ma,' added Pupu who was chomping on a banana.

It was then that Bitan appeared on the scene. He was wearing a pleated dhoti and a singlet and was somewhat tired because of the wedding rituals.

'Why is there so much hullabaloo about this?' he asked as he put on his glasses. 'Pupu will travel with his mother, he will walk into our house holding his mother's hand. Why should he come later? Didn't we do plenty of rituals in the last two days? There's no need for more. Anandi, if you think you don't want to dress like a bride, then don't. Wear whatever you are comfortable in.'

'Happy now? No one has tried to separate your son from you, Anandi,' remarked a relative as soon as Bitan left.

'She is very lucky,' another aunt said. 'I didn't know that a man could be so considerate of a woman's feelings.'

'Prabha-boudi, these modern, educated youngsters are something else!' one more person chimed in. 'Just because I was born a woman doesn't mean I'll have to tolerate being treated badly and being subservient to fathers and husbands. I have seen for myself how times have changed. And it's good, isn't it? Even until a few years ago no one would have dared to think about getting a widow remarried and even if they did, the girl would be made to feel eternally indebted to her new husband and in-laws.'

'No, no. You're from the village and that's why all this is new for you. These days, young city widows remarry quite often. In fact, when their husbands are still alive, they leave them for another man and break up their homes! This is nothing.'

Once the fire is lit, it is not so easy to douse it. All of them knew they were speaking out of turn and saying what shouldn't be said. Still, they could not stop themselves.

Anandi left for her marital home wearing a pink Kanjeevaram sari along with appropriate jewellery and holding Pupu's hand. For most of the journey, Pupu sat on Bitan's lap as the pair chatted away on their way to Kolkata. It was half past twelve when the car arrived in front of Bitan's house. It was a big house built in the traditional style. Until a few generations ago, their family owned the biggest paper mill in eastern India. The business had gone under since then. Bitan and his two brothers were all involved in different businesses and were well established. They still lived in a joint family. Hence, one could say that their past had not yet lost its sheen. They were simply remade by modernity.

So what if it were an old house? It still shone like brand new. The bannister of the staircase that climbed from the ground to the first floor was made of mahogany. The polish on it still glistened. The marble floors were cleaned daily and there was no spot or stain anywhere. The bathrooms had bathtubs, every room had an air conditioner, the verandahs were not made ugly with sarees, petticoats and blouses hanging from the clotheslines. Instead, they were decorated with expensive plants. Bitan's sisters-in-law were highly educated and came from well-to-do families. The house showed a casual display of taste and wealth.

They lived in an older part of the city, and the women of the neighbourhood gathered to have a glimpse of the new bride. But none of them trespassed on the property and invaded the house.

'She's so young ... Her son is still a baby ... How sad ... Still a baby, what does he understand anyway? He'll think of Bitan as his father ... Will he remember his father?' they whispered.

Pupu shot out of Bitan's brother-in-law's lap and ran into the house. Bitan's aunt was the oldest married woman in the family; therefore, it was her duty to welcome Anandi into the house after completing all the rituals. Anandi noticed how violently her hands were shaking—she was unable to hold the prayer tray properly. She could not look at Anandi's face either. She blessed the new bride with great difficulty. She touched her fingers to Anandi's chin, gave her a quick kiss and promptly shuffled aside, relieved. At this moment, Anandi wished she could take a look at Bitan's face but he was pretending he hadn't seen anything and got busy telling everyone to wrap it up quickly. Anandi bowed before the idols of Lakshmi and Narayana, and the photograph of the family guru, touched the feet of all the elders including her mother-in-law before she was finally allowed to sit.

The house was teeming with Bitan's friends and family. No sooner did she sit down than all of them flocked to her, yet she could see the hesitation and doubt written large on their faces. When she had gone to her in-laws' after her wedding to Sutanu, the women of his family had made many playful jokes at her expense.

'You really like your husband, don't you? My my, you have already become such good friends! A love marriage, is it?' They tried to embarrass her with these remarks. Sutanu had intervened by telling everyone Anandi needed to rest. This led to another round of jokes.

'You are already so smitten with her?' a female neighbour asked.

Bitan's family was not interested in these juvenile amusements. 'Do you like the house?' only one of them asked. Meanwhile, 'It's so hot, isn't it? Not the best time to get married,' someone else said.

Anandi did not even pretend to be shy, because honestly, that would be ridiculous. She believed that no matter what, getting married within two years of becoming a widow was already a mark of shamelessness for many people. She had quite willingly accepted another man in place of her husband. She had taken two men as her bedfellows.

'It's late. Has Pupu eaten?' she asked instead.

'Pupu? Who's Pupu?'

'Pupu ... my son.'

'Oh, I see. I have seen him around. Time has flown and it's indeed half past one!'

The room emptied out soon after and everyone got busy looking for Pupu. Anandi was relieved. Bitan's eldest sister-in-law was very sophisticated. She was nearly forty, her hair was cut short, and she was a teacher at an English-medium school.

'You have nothing to worry about. Bitan gave Pupu a bath and the two of them have eaten together,' she said to Anandi sweetly as she came running into the room. 'He is very happy and swinging his legs and chatting away with everyone. He says he can pick bones from fish easily. He's looking for the river and is already curious to know where he'll go to school! He is full of questions. Bitan is very good with kids. I'm sure they're having a good time together. Go on, take a bath. We'll eat together.'

This was how the day went by. It was the first night in her marital home. Like shadows, Anandi was surrounded by people all round the clock. Still, no one really came up to her. In the evening, when the party moved to her mother-in-law's room, she got the feeling that everyone had forgotten about her as they reminisced about old times. She had become invisible. She even had the chance to slip away and make a quick phone call to her parents.

'I'm perfectly fine, Ma. Everyone is very nice,' she said to her mother.

'Pupu? What is he up to?' her mother asked. 'Is he asking for us? I hope he is not crying.'

'Pupu went for a ride with Bitan in his car in the evening. Bitan has bought him a bunch of toys. He is fine,' she answered.

'He ate with the others at the dining table. Didn't throw any tantrums.'

'There are too many new people, so much joy and excitement, he won't ask about you so easily,' she said without thinking too much. 'Let things calm down and he'll be reminded of you. Then see how he cries.'

'I don't know what to do,' her mother said. 'Should I remove Sutanu and your photo from the wall? Bitan and you will visit soon, you'll stay in this room, sleep here. Would it be right to keep Sutanu's photos in the room?'

'Remove them,' she answered.

'What else is there to do?' Her mother started to sob. 'We loved him very much too. I think about him every time I look at Pupu. We're helpless now, as all we want is for Bitan to think of Pupu and you as his own. Sutanu has no place in your new life.'

'You're right, Ma. He has no place here. Bitan is great, Bitan is kind, but did he ever ask me about Sutanu? He has never asked to see Sutanu's photos. He knows Sutanu was a chapter in my life, which is now a thing of the past.'

According to the traditions of this night, Bitan was not supposed to be a part of the party. Pupu was with Bitan all this time. Anandi heard that Pupu was watching TV with his head on Bitan's lap. She also heard that they had eaten together and gone to bed. Pupu had come into her mother-in-law's room looking for her only once in the evening.

'What's this, Pupu?' Anandi wanted to hold Pupu to her breast and say to him, 'You seem to have forgotten your mother ever since you've found your Babai.'

The fact that Pupu would address Bitan as 'Babai' was decided by Bitan. Anandi did not know when this was done. In the morning, while setting off for her marital home she realised that Pupu was already familiar with the term. It brought her great relief because she had often worried about whether Pupu would address Bitan as 'Baba' like he did Sutanu. Her dead husband's face floated into her vision every time the thought struck her. If Pupu called Bitan 'Babai', then there was nothing wrong with it, really. Surely, he wouldn't address him as Uncle or Kaku? Whereas 'Baba' would mean contending for Sutanu's place in his son's life. Weren't they taking away everything from Sutanu little by little? Pupu shouldn't have doubts about the Baba he was born to and the Baba who lived with him. Bitan did not waste a moment before adding an 'i' at the end of the word, and thus preserving Pupu's relationship with Sutanu.

Pupu came into Anandi's mother-in-law's room. By now, all the relatives had accepted the new bride's dual identity as a mother. Pupu was now just Pupu, and not the son of the bride's previous husband. They had started to dote on him—he was a child after all, and a guest. Therefore, as soon as Pupu entered the room, everyone greeted him with smiles.

'Bitan told me he can recite Rabindranath Tagore's poems by heart,' her mother-in-law said. 'Is that true? Recite something for us, please.'

Pupu paid no attention to the request and instead raised his arms towards the tall bed, urging Anandi to lift him up. She experienced a strange stiffness in her limbs; the heavy new saree and jewellery made movement cumbersome. Ultimately, she did not have to do anything. One of Bitan's cousins put Pupu on the bed.

'I want to sleep, Ma,' he said, hugging his mother. 'Put me into my sleeping suit, please.'

'Sleeping suit! What's that now?' someone piped up mockingly.

'A suit you wear to bed,' answered Pupu.

Anandi's sister-in-law was in the room.

'Oh, I know what he's talking about,' she said. 'Come on now, show me where it is.'

Her eldest sister-in-law had one son, a teenager. The other one, who was speaking to Pupu, did not have any children and neither did Bitan's sister and her husband.

'Have you got his sleeping suit?' the sister-in-law asked Anandi.

'My mother must have packed it. Though I'm not sure,' she replied.

Her mother had bought many new clothes for Pupu because he would go with his mother to her new home. Anandi did not know what else she had packed for Pupu.

Pupu left the room soon after and she hadn't seen him for the rest of the evening. It was not very late but by the time Anandi finished eating and went to bed, the men in the house had already fallen asleep. Her sister-in-law showed her to her room.

'Will you be able to sleep alone, Anandi? If not, I can sleep with you,' she said. Had this been her first marriage, her sophisticated sister-in-law would've said to her, *It's just a matter of one night. From tomorrow, you will sleep with your husband!*

'No, I'll be okay,' she said.

'Change out of your clothes and go to bed. I'll wake you up in the morning. Wear a saree then. You'll have to wear one for the next few days—till the relatives keep visiting. After that, you can go back to wearing salwar kameez, or whatever you like. This is an old neighbourhood, married women still don't wear jeans. But the kind of guy Bitan is, he might even tell you to wear Western clothes only. Your mother-in-law won't object to it either.'

Anandi had formed her opinions about Bitan by now. Ever since he was young, he was the liberal type. He opposed the idea of subjecting another person to one's whims and desires and was also against forcing someone to do anything against their will. The more she learnt about him, she felt as though a weight lifted off her. Her eyes became heavy with sleep. She quickly took off her saree and climbed into bed. New surroundings, a new bed; sleep eluded her at first but she eventually fell asleep without realising. In the early hours of the morning when she woke up, she instinctively reached for Pupu on the right side of the bed. For a brief moment, she suspected he had slid towards the edge of the bed in his sleep and was hanging by the mosquito net. But then she realised he wasn't there at all. In fact, Pupu was asleep next to someone called Bitan. This was Bitan's house, and she was sleeping in a room in his house. The Ganga was not visible from here.

The second day after the wedding went by in a blink of an eye. It was the day of the Boubhaat, the bride's first full day in her marital home. People started arriving right from the morning. The shehnai was being played at a low volume. The living room was rearranged for the new bride to take her seat. Make-up artists from a beauty parlour arrived to dress up Anandi. As suggested by her sister-in-law, Anandi picked a Banarasi saree and pinned the anchol to her left shoulder. Instead of wearing ornaments made with fresh flowers, as brides had done for many generations, Anandi pinned some yellow and orange flowers in her hair. They matched the colour of her saree. No one objected. She was on her feet during the festivities and didn't sit on the ornate chair laid out for her. She felt that it was still too early to forget that she was a widow. Moreover, Pupu was around too. These traditions were not in keeping with her reality. Since her chair was empty, it was Pupu who climbed onto and out of it whenever he felt like. She was impressed by Bitan's elegance. He introduced her to those she did not know.

'This is Anandi,' he said simply. 'And this is our son Parambrata,' he added if Pupu was nearby.

As he publicly committed to look after Anandi's well-being, he also asked for Pupu. He served some food on a silver platter and gave Pupu a new set of clothes. 'You are my son. I'll give you whatever you ask for. Alright?' he said to Pupu.

Hearing this, Pupu nodded his head joyfully and began throwing tantrums saying he wanted to eat the food served on the ceremonial plate.

'No, it's too spicy. You won't like it,' the others explained. We have fried a fish for you. You can eat it with us.'

But Pupu would not listen and began crying. The rest of them tried to console him as Pupu noisily gulped back his tears. Anandi looked on helplessly.

'How long should I wait before I can scold Pupu?' she thought to herself.

Pupu was asleep in the chair but his mother hadn't noticed when her child had gone to sleep, tired from causing mischief. However, Bitan did.

'Boudi, Pupu has fallen asleep. Has he eaten?' he asked his sister-in-law.

Pupu started to cry when Anandi's parents left for Chandannagar at half past ten. It had tired him out. Anandi was exhausted too but she continued to smile as she chatted with Bitan's friends and their wives.

'He was sitting at the table with his grandparents. I saw him eating a fish fry,' said Bitan's sister-in-law.

'Anandi, should we wake him up and give him some food?' Bitan said.

'He won't wake up now that he has fallen asleep.'

Bitan picked up the sleeping Pupu, put him to bed, and returned to the party.

The night progressed and the guests began to leave one by one. Anandi sat down to dinner with Bitan and his family. After dinner, she went to her room with her sister-in-law. The bed had been decorated with flowers. Two tall bouquets were placed by the head of the bed while those received from the guests were arranged in one corner of the room. There was no one else with them.

'Here is your room, Anandi. Bitan will come soon,' her sister-in-law said. 'Both of you have a lot to talk about. This is the beginning of your new life as a married couple, after all. Our work here is done. I'll leave now. I'm so tired I feel my bones will break. I'll sleep all day tomorrow!'

Anandi did not expect her sister-in-law to say so little. She listened to her with her head lowered. She didn't ask where Pupu was sleeping. She suspected that Bitan's family would be annoyed if she did so. Of course, if she had seen that Pupu was neglected and not looked after properly, then she could have asked this question even on their first night together as a married couple.

But in the last two days, the warmth shown by Bitan, his brothers, their wives, his sister and her husband, and even his nephew towards Pupu was overwhelming. He was so well taken care of that Pupu did not throw tantrums about wanting to go back to Chandannagar with Anandi's parents. Thus, asking this trivial question would not be appropriate at the moment. Truly, she did not have to worry about Pupu anymore. She had heard Bitan and his brother talk about adopting him legally. She wanted Pupu to take Bitan's surname. If Pupu continued to be a Roy, then Anandi's relationship with her son and her new husband would appear quite peculiar. They would be a family, yes, but the faultlines would still be visible.

And now, standing in this colourfully decorated room, she was reminded of Sutanu. She suspected he was in the room somewhere, hiding from plain sight and looking at her from the corner of his eyes. The family she had built with Sutanu had fallen apart. At this moment, Sutanu, Anandi and Pupu were standing far apart from each other. None of them could make their arms reach for the other.

Bitan entered the room a few minutes later. He shut the door and smiled shyly at her. It did not seem like it was the same Bitan who always had every situation under complete control. 'I'm feeling very nervous now,' Bitan said. 'Don't keep standing there, change your clothes.'

He pulled Anandi into an embrace. He slipped a ring on her finger and murmured in a barely audible voice, 'Now I know why I was so troubled when I saw you for the first time, Khuku. It was because I wanted to have you like this.'

He kissed her deeply and Anandi fell into a trance-like state. It was as if the ground had suddenly slipped from under her feet. Bitan filled the pauses between kisses with things he wanted to say to her. 'I'm totally new to this, Khuku. I know nothing. Teach me everything I should know.'

There was no sarcasm in what he said. It was passion, plain and simple. Until now, Anandi had all sorts of doubts about Bitan while he had wanted her simply for who she was. The words Bitan said to Anandi melded them together because, as someone who had married for the second time, Anandi did not know what initiative she should have taken as a bride on their first night together. She now knew that Bitan had accepted her with a clear conscience and she wrapped herself around him. Her body was discovering anew what the masculine touch felt like. She began to tremble in his arms. Thoughts of Sutanu and Pupu no longer played in her mind.

They both gave themselves to each other on the first night without any hesitation. Bitan received what he wanted, and Anandi had gained something even more valuable. She realised what was missing from her life and what she craved. She was completely enamoured with Bitan now.

Later at night, Anandi woke Bitan up and pulled him towards her. The 'understanding' that her sister-in-law had wanted them to have with each other was successfully established. Anandi knew there were no secrets in this marriage, and neither she nor Bitan had anything to hide from each other. She knew that from here, every night would be a carnival. A fantastic carnival. She sighed deeply and went back to bed as the day broke over the horizon. Bitan had earned her respect and gratitude. She fell deeply in love with him and soon a distance developed between her and Pupu. She left her son with her sister-in-law before leaving for her five-day honeymoon. Each time she spoke to Pupu on the phone, he would cry for her noisily but she was not disconcerted by it. She felt there was much that Bitan deserved from her and she would, from the bottom of her heart, do everything in her capacity to give him what he deserved.

Bitan got busy with work after they returned from the honeymoon. In his free time, he would be eager to go out together as a family to restaurants, cinemas and elsewhere. Anandi had noticed how Bitan would look forward to playing with Pupu after coming home. Pupu, too, was sad on the nights Bitan returned late from work. 'Why isn't Babai home yet? Call him,' he'd ask.

Anandi did not have to behave like a new bride for long. Soon enough, she started to scold Pupu when she needed to and told him scary stories to stop him from being too naughty. She became attentive to her domestic duties. She would often call Bitan and tell him sternly about the things that were needed at home.

'Pupu needs to be taken to the doctor. I hope you haven't forgotten. When are you coming?' she told Bitan when Pupu fell sick.

'Take him yourself if I'm late,' Bitan said.

Bitan showed no insincerity or false display of affection. Anandi knew he would take care of everything; nothing escaped his attention. And, on his behalf, Anandi, too, looked after everyone and everything—Pupu, Bitan's mother and the household.

Still, every now and then, there was one thing that pricked at Anandi's heart like a thorn. Pupu would still sometimes demand to sleep in the room with her. But she could no longer allow it. At first, Pupu threw tantrums, cried loudly, behaved stubbornly. 'I want to sleep next to Ma', he screamed.

His demands would be met by Bitan's silence. Her sisters-in-law would coax and cajole the child and gently take him out of the room.

'My dear, don't you like me? Won't you sleep here in my room? I'll stroke your hair and sing you lullabies in my hoarse voice!' her mother-in-law would say from the other room.

'No, no, I want to sleep with Ma,' Pupu cried even louder.

She waited eagerly for the night—the carnival—just like Bitan.

'It won't be right for a child to witness the things we get up to at night,' Bitan said once when Pupu was crying.

Since then, Anandi could not look at Bitan whenever Pupu threw a tantrum. He made these demands rarely but when he cried at the top of his lungs asking for his mother to let him sleep next to her, an image would float into Anandi's vision where she was stuffing a crumpled Pupu into a small suitcase and no matter how hard she tried, she simply could not zip it properly, which in turn contorted his little body even further.

Anandi had not stayed with her parents in Chandannagar in the six months since she had got married. Bitan hated to let her go. She would go in the morning and come back by the time evening rolled in. Bitan, as well as his family, were not exactly pleased by the possibility of Pupu taking leave from school to visit his maternal grandparents. Anandi rarely visited her parents or stayed with them but now an opportunity had suddenly presented itself. Pupu would be away from school for four days including the weekend. Meanwhile, Anandi's mother was not well either.

'This time I'll stay with them for a few days,' she said to Bitan, putting her hands on her hips.

'Oh, help me, God! How can I say no to you when you talk to me like this,' said Bitan. 'Go then. Stay with them.'

He smiled at her sweetly and kissed her forehead.

'Khuku, tell me honestly, are you happy?' Bitan asked her when she was about to leave the room.

'What sort of a question is this?'

'Tell me, please. Are you happy? Have I been able to show you how much I love Pupu and you?'

'Yes, Bitan. Yes, you have.'

'Put your hand on my heart and tell me you are happy, that you have no regrets ...'

'With my hand on your heart.' She embraced Bitan.

The next day, Anandi left for Chandannagar. Pupu seemed to have forgotten his mother the moment he saw his grandparents. Her mother chatted away happily and showed no signs of stopping. Anandi was tired from listening to her mother talk. She went to sit by the river. Pupu ran around her in circles. Soon, the day made way for the evening and after that, the evening bled into the night. Bitan would not stop calling her. Her mother-in-law also called often to ask after Pupu.

'I want to sleep with my grandmother,' Pupu said during dinner.

'So you will, so you will,' her mother said happily.

'No, Ma. He'll sleep with me,' Anandi interrupted.

Her mother was taken aback by Anandi's tone.

'What's this, Anandi? Why do you sound so angry? she asked. 'Has Pupu done something wrong? Whatever it is, you don't have to scold him so late at night.'

'Can I really sleep with you?' Pupu whispered into her ear.

Anandi nodded. She hung the mosquito net and put Pupu under it. She then unwrapped Sutanu's photo and gave it to Pupu.

'Keep it next to your pillow. I'm coming. Don't fall asleep.'

She switched off her mobile. She showered thoroughly, washed her hair, and slipped into an old nightie. Pupu was looking at the photo with wide eyes.

'Ma? Baba!' Pupu exclaimed as soon as she turned off the light.

'Yes, Pupu. Baba. Your father,' she said.

The moonlight flooded the room from the open windows. Pupu did not lie down. Sitting up straight on the bed, he continued to stare out of the window. 'Come, Pupu. Put your head in my lap,' she said.

'This is how we used to sleep. Isn't that right, Ma?' Pupu hugged her tightly and said.

'And we will for as many days as we are here. You and I will sleep together. Your Baba is here too.'

She kissed Pupu. Taking Sutanu's photo into her hand, she brought her mouth to his forehead and planted another sweet kiss on it.

THE DESIRE TO RUN AWAY

Santanu walked for twenty minutes from Sealdah railway station to arrive at the offices of Modern Printing. He entered Creek Row and crossed the lanes and by-lanes. On the corner of the street stood a three-storey, ancient, bare-bricked, moss-covered house that was the office-cum-factory of Modern Printing. The first floor was used for desktop publishing, accounting, receiving orders and delivering mail. The rear portion of the house was covered by an asbestos roof and encircled by a metal grille—this was the factory. The business was almost on its deathbed. Every morning on his way to the office, Santanu suspected today would be the day when he would see the press's gates padlocked.

The owner, Gurudas-babu, was at least seventy-five years old. His son had a government job at the state secretariat and had never shown any interest in running the old printing press. On top of everything, the owner of the house, Banalata Debi, sent a letter a day to Gurudasbabu about promptly vacating the premises. The house was built on a large plot of land, and the promoters were eager to get hold of it. If Gurudasbabu left the house at this point, then he'd still have something to gain. Or so the promoter, Jagmohan, had assured him. Santanu knew that the printing press had never been a flourishing business.

He had already discussed new jobs at a few different places. He would be out of here as soon as something worked out. He received a salary of only Rs 5,000 per month, and Gurudasbabu could hardly be counted on to dispense the full amount at the right time each month. Just the previous month, he had given Santanu Rs 2,500 in the final week and had promised to give the rest, along with the next month's salary, in the first week of the new month. Needless to say, the same thing happened again. In effect, he had missed an entire month's salary. This had become routine.

Santanu was twenty-three years old. His brother, who was two years younger than him and had no skill or education to speak of, was earning more at a leather factory. He got a daily wage of Rs 250. He was also compensated separately for night shifts. But compared to his brother Pratap, Santanu was a more generous person. He handed over his entire salary to his mother, while Pratap was extremely cunning in matters of money. He also had a soft spot for the latest trends in fashion and was going around with a girl too.

Every night, Santanu would listen to Pratap talking sweetly with her on the phone. He would marry her right away if he could, but their mother had declared that Santanu was to be married first. All he needed was a slightly higher salary and a better job for him to start thinking about marriage. In his village, every man over the age of twenty-two was married. Santanu wanted to get married for a different reason altogether. His mother had raised the two brothers by cooking for other families. His father had run away with another woman many years ago and had set up home with her. His mother had tried very hard to get the brothers a proper education. Santanu had just about managed to pass the school-leaving examinations and Pratap had no interest in attending school after the eighth standard. When the boys were young, their mother used to cook at a house in Kamarpara. An old man at that house had studied Santanu's palm and prophesied that he would make a living out of reading and writing. Santanu, after all, had not turned out to be a menial labourer. He was indeed surrounded by letters all day. He'd sit at an ancient computer and type away beautiful Bengali and English words as he consoled himself by saying that the old man had been right indeed.

His mother was not well at present. He woke up early in the morning, finished all the chores in the house, and took the train to Kolkata. It was all increasingly tiresome. A daughter-in-law would be the perfect antidote and his mother would be relieved from doing the household chores. The daughter-in-law would take care of everything. In fact, even this morning, his mother had talked of marriage while sweeping the front yard.

'Pratap is smarter than you, Santanu. See how nicely he is getting everything in order,' she said.

'How?' Santanu was curious.

He lit the kerosene stove and put two cups of tea to boil for his mother and himself. Pratap had chatted on the phone with Tuni late into the night and was still asleep.

'Pratap is paying for Tuni's school. He will make her take the matriculation exams, then the exams for the twelfth standard, marry her, and find her a job,' his mother answered as she pumped water from the tubewell.

'That's a wonderful plan.'

Santanu was doubtful that his mother understood what either 'wonderful' or 'plan' meant.

'But what I'm trying to say is that Pratap has said that if her family forces her to marry now, then he'll agree to it and bring her home,' his mother continued.

'Let him then.'

'I told him that he could certainly marry her but where is the space for her to stay? I have one room and the other one belongs to you. Will she sleep on the porch? So, Pratap has decided he'll build a room on the western side. How clever Pratap is! Only you have stayed a fool.'

'It's good, isn't it?' she added as she soaked a bed sheet in a bucket, 'Pratap will bring home an educated bride. Instead of lending me a helping hand, I'll have to load up her plate and feed her. I can't even get you married. The job you have doesn't pay anything. Did you ask for this month's salary?'

His mother's voice was still playing in his head when he crossed Creek Row and walked into one of the narrow by-lanes. Then, as was inevitable, he slowed his pace as he walked by a dilapidated two-storeyed house. He opened his eyes wide and stared intently at the broken windows of the second floor. No one was at the window then, but a woman drifted into sight no sooner than he had lifted his eyes upwards. Her pale, slim fingers rested on the wooden frame of the window. She leaned heavily across it as though she would jump any moment. God from which secret corner she saw him entering the lane! Every day, no matter what, she would appear in front of him as soon as he arrived under her window. Every day on his way to work, while going home from work, and for some reason during breaks when he stood outside the house, he would lift his eyes and she would appear. Santanu had got used to this weird little game that they had been playing for the last two or three months. Nowadays, he would even dream about her when asleep. He woke up as soon as she appeared in his dreams. He took the mirror that his mother had brought home from one of the houses she worked in, one that had developed a hairline crack in the jostling crowd of the train and took a good look at his reflection. What an odd face he had! It was neither long nor round. His cheeks were pointed and pockmarked, his eyes small. And more importantly, even the most cursory look at him revealed that he belonged to a poor family. A country bumpkin. He still put oil in his hair and was oblivious to fashion trends. Meanwhile, Pratap's flashy clothes and cheap accessories were enough to mark him out as a desirable groom. And yet, the girl waited for him every day. Why? A city girl as fair-complexioned as her and with lovely hair that fell to her shoulders.

The girl could not have been more than nineteen years old. She was supposed to be studying at a school or college but she was always home during the time when classes were in session. Santanu often wondered about it but he knew no one would answer his questions. He could not stop himself from sneaking glances at the girl. A long, pointed face, big eyes. Santanu decided he would sometimes stroll into this lane to look at her.

However, something unexpected happened that morning when Santanu arrived at his usual spot under the window. A paper drifted from the girl's hand. He reached for it and grabbed it.

'In front of the church. 3.30 p.m.,' said the note.

Still holding the paper in his hands, Santanu stared mutely at the window. Right then, someone called the girl. She answered and ran off inside. Santanu carefully folded the paper and stuffed it into his pocket. Sitting in front of the computer at Modern Printing, his heart was not in it. Why did the girl want to meet him? Had she fallen in love with him? Did exchanging glances every day do the trick? She knew nothing about him. And what was it about him that would make a woman fall in love with him? How could a city girl of a decent family find him attractive?

Santanu's blood began to boil. The church? Where was it anyway? He wasn't aware of any church. What would happen now? In front of which church would she be waiting for him at three-thirty in the afternoon? Today? She hadn't mentioned the day. How would Santanu know?

He could not focus on work. There was another man at the office who was the same age as Santanu; his name was Sameer. Sameer was the cunning type. He was always prepared for every situation. He pressed his black, parched lips together and smiled slyly. 'Is there a church around here?' Santanu asked him.

'There's one on Lenin Sarani. Why do you ask?' said Sameer.

'For no reason really,' Santanu said with a small smile.

'Don't fuck with me! Tell me why!' Sameer was not ready to let it go. Though Santanu intended to tell Sameer only a little, he eventually ended up confessing the entire matter.

'Arrey, her! She's damn beautiful,' Sameer said.

'I'm scared. Should I go? Are you sure? Would it be right?'

'Of course, you should. What will she do anyway? Will she kidnap you? Plus, I will come with you. I'll hide myself. Let's see what she says!'

Sameer and Santanu reached the church at quarter past three. After waiting a short while, they saw the girl timidly making her way towards them from behind the church. She was wearing a salwar kameez with a white floral print and a blue-coloured dupatta. She anxiously cast her eyes in every direction as she walked. It was the first time Santanu was seeing more than her face. She was extremely skinny yet graceful. Village girls were usually bereft of such qualities. Why did the girl want to see him? Santanu felt twice as nervous—he wanted to exit the scene but Sameer clasped his hands tightly. The girl quickly covered her head with her dupatta as soon as she arrived in front of them.

'I'm done for!' she said. 'The main door shuts if anyone pulls it from outside. I put a stick against the hinges but a gust of wind has dislodged it. How will I get in now? I'll get a good thrashing for leaving the house.'

The girl's eyes welled up. Santanu did not know what to say to her.

'Why will they beat you? What's wrong with going out?' Sameer remarked.

'It's a long story! My parents are dead, that's why my uncle and aunt beat me so much. They want to marry me off quickly so they can get some money for it. But I don't want to marry the man they have picked for me.' The girl's face fell. 'I have been in love with you for a long time.' She looked at Santanu after saying this.

A maelstrom of emotions stirred in Santanu's heart. No one had ever confessed their love for him. *I have been in love with you for a long time!* Santanu could barely breathe and he was glad to have Sameer with him during this momentous event.

'So, what will happen now?' said Sameer.

'I won't go home. I won't, I won't. I decided on my way here,' the girl said.

'What?' said Sameer.

'I'll run away with you,' the girl told Santanu.

'What? What do you mean by run away with me?' Santanu somehow managed to reply.

'What does this mean! How can you just run away?' Sameer butted in.

'Why not?' the girl asked. 'Won't you be able to feed me? You have a job, don't you?'

'Hey, what's your name?' said Sameer.

'Riya.'

'Riya, you know nothing about him and you want to run away with him?'

'Didn't I just say I love him?' Riya said and twisted her face stubbornly.

A protest march snaked its way through Lenin Sarani. Santanu felt an awful itch to slink out of there and become one with the crowd. But he was reminded once again that the girl was in love with him! The girl was in trouble. What if her uncle and aunt really thrashed her black and blue when she returned home? What then? In that moment, he too had fallen in love with the helpless girl. As far as Santanu was concerned, her confession was a command for him. What kind of man would he be if he failed to protect the one who was in love with him? Sameer was better looking than him, more refined too, but the girl had eyes only for Santanu. At twenty-three, Santanu could not imagine anything better happening to him. He made his decision. 'I'm Santanu,' he said. 'My mother works as a cook at other people's homes. My home is in a village called Piyali. We are quite poor but I should not have trouble feeding you. Will you be able to adjust to this life?'

'How far is your village?' the girl asked.

'An hour and a half from Sealdah.'

'Wonderful. My uncle will never be able to find me.'

'I won't have anything to do with this,' Sameer said. 'I'll go now. I don't want to get in trouble with the police. Santanu, find out if she's at least eighteen.'

'I'm seventeen,' the girl clarified.

'Oh, fuck!' Sameer exclaimed. 'Santanu, don't do anything without thinking.'

'Why are you scaring him?' said Riya.

'And what about when everyone finds out about you two? Sameer said. 'He'll still have to come here for work. Won't he get a sound thrashing?'

'Why don't you let it be? We'll sort it out,' said Santanu.

Riya came up with a plan.

'Why don't we go to a temple and get married right away? No one will be able to separate us then! Not even the police's godforsaken father. I'll be eighteen in two months. I won't leave the house in the meantime. I'll stay hidden.'

'Do you still want to run away with me?' asked Santanu.

'What other choice do I have? You should marry me right now. All I need is vermilion in my hair to become your bride!'

'Bride?' Santanu said, shivering.

He thought about how highly regarded he would be in the village if he married someone like her. Smart, beautiful, a city girl who was not afraid to look men in the eyes. How high her eyebrows climbed when she talked to him! A marriage would be good for her. Santanu could not imagine what she would look like in a red saree. He smiled to himself. Would he really get married before his brother?

'Brother, do me a favour,' Santanu said to Sameer. 'Get us married. My mother won't hesitate to take her in as long as she's my bride.'

'Do whatever the fuck you feel like but don't get me involved.'

'Sameer-da, please,' Riya pleaded. 'Can't you do your friend this small favour? And am I not like your younger sister?'

'For fuck's sake! There'll be a lot of trouble,' Sameer ran his fingers through his hair. He rang someone.

'Come to Bowbazar Kalibari. Have to get someone married,' he instructed. Sameer looked dead serious.

An hour later, Santanu put vermilion in Riya's hair and the two of them became a married couple. Riya's wrists were circled with red bangles from the temple and a garland of rajanigandha buds hung from her neck. Riya smiled widely as she fingered the buds. The smile turned into a tinkling laugh. Santanu was enchanted. He became increasingly restless to present his new wife to the village, his mother and Pratap. He could not wait another moment. Sameer, his two friends Chanchal and Rajesh, Santanu and Riya went to an air-conditioned sweetshop to celebrate. Sameer was suddenly transformed into a responsible person of the groom's party.

'I was so worried. This air-conditioned room is a big relief,' Riya said.

'There's no electricity at home. No gas cylinder. No taps. We store water in drums,' Santanu said.

'No electricity?' Riya's eyes were wide with surprise.

Sameer's phone began to ring right then. He took the call, said something, and hung up. 'Bibhas-da is looking for us. He sounds pissed off. Will you go to the office now? I have to ...'

'How can I leave Riya behind?' said Santanu.

Riya was looking at her reflection in the mirror while washing her hands in the basin at the sweetshop. Her face looked somewhat serious.

'Will you not go to this office anymore? Will you quit?' she said.

'Why? How will they know you have eloped with me?'

'You should go to the office, then.'

'What about you?' Santanu was dutifully playing the husband's role.

'I'll wander around for a bit. You can meet me after work.'

'How's that possible? A girl wandering all alone ...'

'Let's do one thing, then,' Riya said while pulling at his shirt. 'I'll wipe off the vermilion and go home. Let them beat me up if they want to! I'll run away again after a week or so. Won't you be able to arrange for an electricity connection by then?'

'In a week?'

'See, the man I was supposed to get married to had AC in his home. But I wanted to elope. Ever since I was a little girl! Even a fan will do. Moreover, there are snakes and whatnot in villages. I'll be scared without lights.'

The sugary syrup from the sweets coated Santanu's lips thickly.

'Won't you be able to do it?' Riya continued.

'I don't know!'

He pulled out a hundred rupees from his pocket and paid for the sweets. He did not wipe the syrup clinging to his mouth.

Sameer asked him to hurry up before dashing out of the shop with his friends. Riya gave the garland to him to hold. She slipped the bangles off her wrists and stuffed them into his pockets. Her slim, soft fingers brushed against him. Leaning on the basin, she quickly washed off the vermilion but did not take her eyes off him.

'Oh, they've got soap too!' she said, smiling playfully at him.

Santanu explained the situation to Sameer as the two of them walked back to Modern Printing.

'Oh damn, oh damn!' said Sameer over and over again.

On entering the office, Santanu saw Bibhas-da standing next to a slim, fair-complexioned, bespectacled man. 'Everyone's in the neighbourhood saying that his niece has run away with Sameer!' Bibhas-da exclaimed as soon as he saw the pair.

'Not me. With him', Sameer took a long look at Santanu from head to toe and said. 'But the girl is already back home.'

'Already back home?'

The man stood up.

'Yep. Your niece has a loose screw in her head!'

'Ah!'

'Go to the police if you like,' Sameer said, though he wanted to say something more. 'Do whatever you want.'

The gentleman lowered his eyes in embarrassment.

'She has run away so many times that the police refuse to write a missing report anymore,' he said, looking at Santanu. 'They laugh at us instead.'

'Want to say something? Sameer said to Santanu, losing his cool. 'If I were you, I'd ask for my three hundred rupees back.'

'No,' answered Santanu.

'She's addicted to running away!' the gentleman added. 'She runs away, puts vermilion in her hair, then wipes it off and comes back home. "Kaka, the guy is a brute. Take me home," she calls me and says. At other times, she says, "Kaka, I miss you already."'

FEAR

It took Rupali exactly two months to realise that she and Gautam had split up. The fact that it had indeed happened dawned on her—not on the first day, not the second, but on the third day when she was putting on make-up before going out with Shatadal in the evening.

Rupali was trapped in a relationship that refused to end. It was like a fish stuck to the hook of a fishing rod. It could only understand a couple of words. Easy enough. But only those who had been through the ordeal knew how hard it was. A curved iron hook was stuck permanently in her throat.

Today, standing in front of the mirror, all of a sudden, a wide smile spread across her face. She had been unable to come out of the doomed relationship for a long time. She was scared for herself. It was the fear of baring her heart in vain. She could not see the new life waiting for her when she walked out of the relationship, and because she could not see this, she spent all her time arguing and feeling angry. When she put an end to it and decided she would no longer be a part of the sordid affair, it led to a feeling of incredible arrogance. It was as though she had just emerged from the pits of hell. Perhaps she deserved to flash a smile, after all.

Rupali's smiling face conveyed this and more. She put on a bit more make-up without thinking too much about it. 'Ma, I'm off!' she said to her mother.

'How beautiful you look,' her mother said, taking a long look at her. 'Go on, just see for yourself. Look at what you are now and what you had become. There were dark circles under your eyes from crying all night long. You had stopped eating. You had no respect for yourself. So well-educated, a good job and you were still taken for a ride. Let it be, I don't want to bring up old memories. Be sure to invite Shatadal in when you're home. I have made kheer.'

'I will,' she answered. 'I won't even have to ask him. He's not the kind to drop me home and slink away!'

'That's good. If a man decides to spend his life with a special woman, he'll try his best to have a cordial relationship with her family. Casual relationships take place inside dark taxis, friends' flats and poorly lit streets. Get it? Then again, Gautam was hardly husband material.'

'Ma, let me tell you something. Gautam didn't even try to hold me back. It was I who was refusing to let him go. I don't want to blame him, really. If anyone's to blame, it's me. I regret that I wasted his time.'

Rupali's mother managed the family business after her husband's death. So what if she just sold sarees? It was still a business, wasn't it? The shop, named after Rupali and located in South Kolkata's Jodhpur Park, was very well-known in the area. You could even call it a boutique if you liked. Her mother went everywhere, getting the weavers to weave sarees according to her instructions and designs. Phulia, Shantipur, Bolpur. And Dhaka, Tangail too, in Bangladesh! The business was doing really well. It was not unusual for 'Rupali' to sell a couple of sarees worth Rs 40,000 every month. Rupali had already told her mother that she would wear a similarly expensive red-and-yellow Dhakai saree on her wedding day.

This evening too, she was wearing a saree from her mother's boutique. A plain cotton saree in yellow with red and blue borders. She looked beautiful. Rupali hailed a taxi. It took her no more than twenty minutes to reach Deshapriya Park. There was a club next door. Shatadal had become a member last year but back then, Rupali knew nothing of Shatadal Lahiri's existence. She entered the club, walked up to the second-floor lounge, and picked a table facing the swimming pool. Shatadal had texted her telling her to make herself comfortable and that he would be there in five minutes.

It was summer, and children and old men were splashing around in the pool. Before long, Rupali was lost in thought, looking at the merrymakers in the water. She thought about how she finally felt no sadness for Gautam. This realisation, which came to her time and again, made her happy. How was she to describe this feeling? It was perhaps exactly how the Harvard MBA graduates felt whenever they thought about their degree languishing safely in their locker. It was a fabulous achievement! On the third date, the two of them had gone for dinner at a Bengali restaurant on Elgin Road after spending some time at the club.

'Rupali, have you given any thought to getting married?' Shatadal asked as they ate.

'No, I mean, till now …,' she lowered her head and replied.

'Do you think we should wait a few more months? Should we go out for at least a year before marrying?'

'Yes, I do. It'll be too soon otherwise.'

'My sister said the same thing too. People get married right away without thinking, but when the time comes, they find it impossible to live with each other. They get divorced soon after. I see this happening all the time. That's why I'm so scared of getting married!'

Rupali's face fell a little. 'I know marriage has become very scary but it's still great,' she said, staring intently at her food-smeared fingers. 'Those who know this try their hardest to keep their marriage alive.'

'I don't like the idea of working hard to keep a relationship going. Love and compromise should be enough to keep a marriage alive. Both husband and wife have to play an equal role in this. It's not right to find faults with each other like a school-teacher. One must remember that they are both individual beings. They grew up differently; their environment and experiences have made them the way they are,' replied Shatadal.

'Sometimes the husband and wife do not have anything in common, they do not understand each other, but to not hurt egos and maintain the status quo, they think of marriage as a great institution that they must preserve,' Rupali said. 'For instance, someone I know said to me, "I have noticed my daughter doesn't keep well when my wife isn't happy. She misses school, doesn't go to her table tennis classes, does poorly in exams. Home feels suffocating because of constant bickering with the maids and the tasteless cooking. It affects me a lot. That's why I try my best to keep the missus happy!"'

After saying this, Rupali looked stupidly at Shatadal, fearing she had inadvertently told him all the reasons why people were afraid of getting married.

'Looking after someone's well-being so *mechanically* is like having an invisible noose around your neck, isn't it?' said Shatadal, taken by surprise.

From a secret corner, somewhere deep inside her, a thin stream of water made her eyes well up and sting. Shatadal did not notice it.

'I asked my friend many times if he took care of his wife without really loving her,' Rupali said. 'Was everything carefully calculated? My friend said he doesn't know!'

'Sorry, but I can't be that kind of husband,' Shatadal said. 'I can't do these asinine things. That's why we shouldn't even think of having babies until at least four years of being married. In fact, we should only have a child when we are sure that, despite our differences, we still see the good in each other. And, if I can be bold, that we still love each other.'

'What are you saying! I'm already thirty,' exclaimed Rupali. 'The marriage will happen one year from now, and a baby, four years after that. When I'm thirty-five! No, no, when will I raise it? I'll be a grey-haired oldie by the time the kid finishes school! No, no, I can't allow that.'

On the third date, Rupali and Shatadal's relationship, if it could be called a relationship, reached a stage when it was no longer formal. There was some intimacy to it. They would get married and have babies. What was unsaid in these talks was the eventuality of two bodies becoming one and sexual pleasure. A wave of delight rose in the heart when one thought about taking the man sitting in front of them or having the woman across the table. Shatadal and Rupali felt a similar thrill as she continued to speak.

'Plus, raising a kid is like running tracks with the agility of an Olympic gymnast. We won't have the tenacity in old age. I see this at school all the time. Twenty-four and twenty-five-year-old parents dart around like a bolt of lightning to get their kids' homework, exams and EC done!'

'What's EC?'

'Extra-curricular.'

'Oh!'

'I know first-hand that raising a future-ready kid is a very difficult and demanding job.'

Rupali fell silent. She saw Shatadal looking at her with a teasing gaze, a smile lingering on his lips. After finishing dinner, while walking together the short distance to the car, Shatadal gingerly took Rupali's hand into his. He dropped her off at home and had a quick chat with her mother, but before he left, he sneaked a kiss on Rupali's cheek at the staircase landing.

Climbing back to the second floor and standing in front of her mother with a wide grin on her face, Rupali thought once more about how her relationship with Gautam was purely physical and, therefore, superficial.

'No matter what happens between us, even if you end things, I will still spend the rest of my days as yours. My heart, my soul—everything is yours!' she had said to Gautam. Now, she was surprised that she had said so.

Even though she was looking at her mother, Rupali smiled triumphantly only for herself. What she had said to Gautam that day was an acceptance of defeat. But today, Shatadal's kiss made her heart bloom like a thousand flowers. It was a declaration of victory. For the first time since her relationship with Gautam ended, she realised she still had hopes of a happy life.

'Shatadal brought up marriage today,' she told her mother before going to bed. 'You may tell Falguni-mashi that we'll marry. Exactly a year from now!'

Her mother called Falguni-mashi without wasting a moment. Shatadal was her sister-in-law's son. That was how Rupali and Shatadal had found each other.

Everything was fine until this point. The fourth, fifth and tenth dates confirmed that Shatadal and Rupali's chemistry was perfect. The biggest common factor between the two was that they both believed they did not have to spread themselves thin to live happily in this vast world. They preferred a quiet life. Neither believed that there was only one sure-shot way to happiness. Also, both of them loved to speak in Bangla, even though Rupali was an English teacher at an English-medium school. Shatadal worked at a fancy corporate job, but Bangla was the preferred language for their private communication. Many such discoveries were made on their dates and during the phone calls throughout the day. Rupali's day started with thinking about Shatadal, and as far as she was concerned, it was the true sign of love. She knew this because it had been the same with Gautam.

The two of them turned up on College Street on a Saturday at the end of a late afternoon stroll. Both of them had studied at City College. It was almost evening by the time they walked down the stairs of the Indian Coffee House after having coffee and a chicken omelette, and walking around the street buying books. The car was parked at some distance. The two of them made their way to Amherst Street.

'I need to withdraw some cash. Wait here, I'll get the money,' Shatadal said when he took a left from the roundabout and saw an ATM. Rupali stood on the footpath as he pushed the glass door and entered the booth.

Rupali turned around to look at the street. On her left, she saw a woman selling jasmine bouquets. She did not know what came over her but she bought ten rupees' worth of flowers for herself and deeply inhaled their sweet fragrance. While walking back to the ATM, she spotted Rani out of the blue and immediately turned to stone.

Rani had her back turned to Rupali. But Rupali had observed her so many times, covertly but carefully, that she could recognise her even in total darkness or a crowd of people. Rani! What was she up to these days? Was Gautam around too? What was Rani doing in front of an ATM booth on Amherst Street in North Kolkata?

Rupali took a quick look to see if Gautam was indeed around. She couldn't see him.

'Let's go,' said Shatadal as he emerged from the booth.

It was at this moment that Rani turned around. Rupali was stunned to see that the woman wearing the kalamkari saree wasn't her! It was a completely different person. They were not alike in any way. Then why did Rupali, without any real reason, think it was her? Just because she was wearing a kalamkari saree? Rani had once told her how much she liked those sarees.

She and Shatadal were together till ten o'clock at night. They ate dinner but Rupali could not stop thinking about how her eyes had deceived her. Worse still, she could not forget how terrified she had felt upon seeing Rani. What was she so scared of?

Rupali was transported back to the days of her relationship with Gautam. Rani did not know anything about it. In front of her, Rupali and Gautam were merely friends despite the age gap. Correction, very good friends. That's why she would often drop in at Gautam's home. They would hang out in his study. That was how willingly (or unwillingly), she had become friends with Rani. At times, she even had to break up their petty fights. It was rather hilarious. She would take Rani's side each time.

'See, she is on my team even though she's your friend!' Rani laughed loudly and said. 'The bond between two women is unbreakable!'

'Not at all! I'm not just Gautam's friend but yours too. I like you very much!' Rupali would act coquettish and declare.

'What's so great about me? I'm just a good-for-nothing housewife!' said Rani.

'Oh no, why do you say that? There is something likeable in every one of us,' Rupali said, hoping to sound wiser than she was.

But she suspected she felt a similar need to please Rani as she did Gautam if only to keep seeing him freely. Rani neither objected to nor suspected anything when Rupali stayed late in Gautam's room chatting with him or visited him when Rani was not around.

So, when Gautam had a seminar and Rani couldn't go because of their daughter's examinations, Rupali went along instead. Gautam would read his new work and because Rani was busy, Rupali would listen to him with an appropriately serious face.

When Rani wasn't home or in the shower, Gautam would pull Rupali onto the divan. For all these stolen moments of togetherness, happiness and affection, it was necessary to stay in Rani's good books and become her friend, make her feel valued, and to keep her happy no matter what.

'What a dreadful man your husband is, Rani!' Rupali said after a particularly good session in bed when Rani came into the room suddenly. 'The great writer won't talk to me if I don't lavish his work with praise. You tell me, can every piece of writing be equally brilliant?'

'Is the gentleman angry because you didn't like what he has written?' Rani said. 'The thing is, you are special to him. He does not want to hear any criticism from you!'

'It's your anniversary today! How many years has it been?' Rupali said one day.

'Ten!'

'So why are we still here? Where's the party? Let's go out for dinner!'

'Let it be! Gautam doesn't even remember we got married on this day all those years ago,' Rani answered.

'I remember the night after the wedding better,' Gautam said hearing this and embraced Rani in front of Rupali. 'That's the real deal, isn't it? Having you all to myself?'

'My goodness, such lovebirds!', Rupali exclaimed and let out a high-pitched giggle to play along and make Rani happy.

'Let me go! Can't think about anything else!' Rani said. 'Gautam is very cunning, Rupali. He forgets our anniversary every year and brings up the wedding night to pacify me! He tells me to take a shower, wear something nice, put on some make-up and spray some perfume. Then he gives me a drink or two before keeping me up all night,' Rani lowered her voice and continued. 'It's been ten years! Should we still be behaving like this? You tell me!'

Rupali's ears and scalp were on fire as she listened to Rani's chatter. Later, she grabbed Gautam by the collar. 'You're still involved with her?' she asked. 'How can you do this? Even the thought of someone else fucking me is enough to kill me.'

'I have to ensure everything looks normal. Or else this arrangement won't work,' Gautam told her. 'My daughter will be hurt. If I don't get Rani into bed at least once a week, she'll be pissed off. There will be arguments and the air will turn foul. Titli will be sad and she won't study or go to school. She'll do poorly in her exams and so, my work, our relationship …' Gautam would sing the same tune each time. There was nothing else to say, anyway.

Rani was an equal participant in Rupali's three-year clandestine relationship with Gautam. But the truth was Rani struck terror in her heart. Still, ignoring it, she had to pretend to be friends with her. Rani was who she wanted to be. In front of her, Rupali was a fool, a simpleton, a nobody, the other woman. Gautam had put her through this to be the good guy and she had followed his instructions, thinking nothing of her self-respect.

Rupali did not say a word to her mother after Shatadal dropped her off at home. She took a long shower. Suddenly, she felt drained of energy. As though she hadn't just come back after having a great time with Shatadal but had spent hour after hour walking on the smelly grounds of the dump yard.

Lying on her bed, Rupali thought to herself that while she had indeed been terrified of Rani and had nightmares about her, why had these feelings not gone away yet? Was Rani still a part of her life? Why was she hallucinating about her? Why was she so surprised when she thought she had seen her? She was done with Gautam. So why couldn't she leave Rani behind?

Rupali couldn't sleep that night. She stayed up thinking about how she could free herself from Rani's clutches. Was it possible at all?

Still deep in thought, she called Shatadal in the early hours of the morning. The phone rang three times before he picked it up.

'What's up, Rupali? What's wrong?' he said in a voice heavy with sleep.

'Since everything is fine, can we get married right away? The thing is my mother is becoming desperate, I wanted to wait a little, give it some time, but my mother …'

'Did you have an argument with your mother? You sound different. Didn't you sleep at all?'

'Yes …'

'Okay. See you in the evening. We'll talk about it then. Alright? Get some sleep now,' said Shatadal.

A month and a half after this, Shatadal and Rupali registered their marriage. Shatadal's home was in Tollygunge. An old house. He renovated the third floor before bringing his new bride home. It was decided that a wedding ceremony would take place six months later. Rupali continued to live in her Jodhpur Park home even after being legally married to Shatadal. He dropped in often. They hadn't been fully intimate yet. Both were saving themselves for the night after the wedding.

There were only two months to go. Rupali's mother had started shopping for the wedding. Rupali would get married in a red Banarasi saree. She wanted to buy a new pair of shoes and so, she went to a mall on Elgin Road by herself. It was almost eight in the evening when she was done. She made her way to Rowland Road to get a taxi when all of a sudden, she saw Rani in front of her.

This was completely unexpected. Her heart beat loudly against her chest. She thought about whether it was another illusion. But why was she still so scared of Rani? She was no longer an outsider in someone's life, no longer the other woman. She was getting married to a well-established, well-liked, kind man. She was the centre of his world. Then, why the fear? Why did Rani still scare her so? Her heart crumpled in her chest as misgivings ravaged her. And now, Rani was in front of her! She wanted to sprint to the other side of the road.

'Rupali?' said the person who looked exactly like Rani.

She was stunned. Was it indeed her?

'Yes?' she answered in a timid whisper.

'Can't you recognise me? Have you already forgotten me in these six months?'

'No, no, no, not at all!'

'I saw you before but I was quite sure I was mistaken. In fact, this has already happened a few times!'

'What do you mean?'

'I mean, I often seem to see you on the streets. Whenever I see a young, slim, beautiful, fresh-faced young woman, I immediately assume it's you. Though, of course, I realise my mistake right away too. It made me feel so scared, my heart would start beating like mad!'

'Afraid? Of me? Why?' Rupali's throat felt like sandpaper.

'I used to be very scared of you, Rupali, though I never let it be known. I worried my life would fall apart if you or anyone else got a whiff of how terrified I was. I would pray to God that one day you'd leave Gautam. It's true you have gone your way but I still can't seem to shake off the fear. It crouches quietly in my subconsciousness. It looks like you. Will this fear ever leave me alone? Perhaps not ...'

Rani lightly grazed Rupali's skin. Rupali extended her fingers too. The two women, without any apprehension, felt—truly felt—their fears for the first time.

HALLUCINATION

'Rani, you have to come. I won't eat if you don't.' For the last few days, her mother had called every day and said, 'I will make boiled vegetables for you. You have to come to eat. I'll ask Khagen to get some curd. After lunch, you'll lie down next to me. I'll make tea for you in the evening and you can leave after that. The way he spoke to me in my dreams ...'

And then her mother burst into tears in a way that only old men and women can. A strange sound. It sounded like a cough at first, but once the crying started, it appeared as though she had been holding back tears for nearly a century. It was as though an ancient glacier had cracked and given way to a ferocious stream. And then, she worried that her mother would asphyxiate and die if she carried on crying in this manner. When her mother started to cry, she on one side and her sister-in-law on the other, both tried desperately to stop her.

'Ma, Ma! I am very hurt. I have spent thirty years in this house and you still don't think of me as your daughter!' Rani heard her sister-in-law say.

'Bouma, why do you say that?' her mother answered through tears. She was taken aback. Rani could hear everything on the other side.

'You've never cried for me like this, have you? Even when I was almost dying. I have never seen you cry for me!'

Rani suspected her sister-in-law was not joking this time. There was a trace of accusation and sorrow in what she was saying. She feared her sister-in-law would also start crying soon.

'Bouma, he came in my dreams and told me clearly that Rani—'

'I know, Ma. You told me about it as soon as you woke up.'

'It was not me speaking. It was him. This is his wish. Aha, what's all this! I have been told to feed Rani boiled vegetables. The vegetables should not be cut into small pieces. How can I take on such a big responsibility? On top of that, he said to me, "Mejobou, you can't be trusted to get anything done." You won't believe how angry that made me. He left when the kids were only this tall. Didn't I raise them, holding them to my breast? All he did was stare mutely from afar. That's why he's been haunting my dreams and ordering me to get hold of Rani and feed her boiled vegetables. Bouma, why don't you ask Rani to come? She's going on about her son and says she can't come because of him!'

'Rani, my dear, forget everything and come here and eat your boiled vegetables,' like each time, this time too, her sister-in-law grabbed the phone and said. 'Or else your mother will lose her mind! She's already going crazy about this.'

'Rani, I don't feel good about this,' she then lowered her voice and added. 'She's very flustered. Every day she dreams about her husband. My dear, don't forget to drop in soon.'

Rani would go. Of course, she would. How could she not! It was just that the first time her mother had called, she had let slip that she would be visiting Bappa's girlfriend Razia. Since then, her mother had worried that Rani would not come to see her. Just like she had not at other times, even though she had promised she would. She thought that Rani would play the same trick on her again.

She promised her sister-in-law she'd come.

'Boudi, talk some sense into Ma. I'll arrive before noon but I have to leave by four. Razia's house is in the extreme south of the city. In South City, actually! You can imagine how long it will take to travel from Baranagar.'

'Rani, can you imagine!' her sister-in-law said. 'Even your son is ready to bring home a bride.'

'Don't know if she'll be his bride, Boudi. You know what the times are like! Now they are all over each other, and the next moment, they will break it off. Don't you remember what happened to Sarthak-da's daughter? She was in a live-in relationship for three years before calling it off and agreeing to an arranged marriage. I have told Bappa, "You had two girlfriends before her. I don't know if this Razia will last either. What's the need to get the families involved right now? Didn't you say you're not interested in getting married!"'

'So, why are you visiting her family then?' asked her sister-in-law.

'How can I turn down an invitation? Her parents have invited me.'

'It's normal for the girl's parents to be serious about things like this. No matter how modern we think we are. Anyway, come when you can. I have a lot to tell you.'

Rani did not waste any time on Wednesday. She reached Baranagar from Hazra Road well before noon. This house used to be full of life once upon a time. Her uncles and aunts, all used to live here with their families. Now, only her youngest uncle was alive. The rest of the house was occupied by her mother, her brother and his wife, and their son Baban and his wife. Moreover, Baban's wife did not really live there. Baban was Rani's brother Jayabrata's only son. Her cousins lived in Baranagar but had moved out of the family home. None of them had really left their home turf and only two had shifted to Kolkata. They did not want to live in Baranagar anymore. The maid, Shyama, opened the door. Sunlight washed over the verandah on her uncle's side. The portion of the house that belonged to her brother had been whitewashed for Baban's wedding. It hadn't even been a year since then. Rani finally had the chance to visit her mother after nearly three months. Back in the day, her mother and aunts would observe every festival at home. Saraswati puja, Lakshmi puja, Annapurna puja, but now, all celebrations barring Lakshmi puja had ceased. Her mother and sister-in-law were waiting for her on the staircase as though she needed to be shown the way and welcomed in properly.

'Hey, why are you standing here like this?' Rani laughed and said. 'Am I the prime minister visiting from Delhi?'

Her mother opened her mouth and her dentures flashed in a wide smile.

'Oh Rani, isn't that true!' her sister-in-law said. 'Not the prime minister but the president. We had to fall at your feet to get you to visit us.'

Her sister-in-law was tall and still slim, and had a formidable personality. Rani had an easy relationship with her and the two understood each other quite well. It was quite rare to see such friendship in most families. Rani laughed loudly.

'Oh, don't you know?' she said. 'I'm the newest president of the cultural wing of the local women's club!'

'Oh, is that so!'

Her mother laughed with such glee as though she had been waiting all her life for Rani to achieve something as spectacular as being elected the president of the cultural wing of the local women's club. Rani wanted to laugh at her mother's doings but her eyes filled with tears instead. What a pure heart her mother's generation had!

'Just wait and watch what happens! I'll call every VIP to tea,' she said.

'May you do great things in life,' her mother said and touched her chin affectionately. 'Go in, and thank the gods first.'

Her sister-in-law burst into a peal of laughter.

'Jealous of my epic success, are you?' Rani remarked.

Being in her maternal home instantly made Rani feel many years younger. She was no longer a perimenopausal woman touching fifty or the mother of a twenty-five-year-old man. She felt like a young girl with pigtails, a Bollywood junkie, who lived in Rathin Ghosh Lane in Baranagar!

The hours went by in the blink of an eye. Her sister-in-law got busy with chores around the house. Rani lay down on her mother's ancient bed and rolled around on the cool mattress as the two of them chatted together. Her mother was yet again recalling the dream she had had in excruciating detail. How her dead husband appeared in front of her, how he threatened his wife, asked about Rani, instructed that boiled vegetables be given to her and so on. Rani's eyes were transfixed on her father's dusty black-and-white photograph hanging on the wall.

'Ma, give me Baba's photo, please,' she said, coming out of her reverie. 'I'll see if I can get a colour copy.'

No sooner was she done speaking than she realised there was no point in fixing the image now or framing it anew. The movie was over and the credits had rolled too. The audience was preparing to leave the hall. No one was going to break their heads discussing the beautiful calligraphy in which 'The End' was written. Her mother did not answer her and promptly changed the topic to Bappa's girlfriend, Razia.

'What did you want to talk about, Boudi?' Rani asked her sister-in-law after lunch when her mother had drifted off to sleep. Her sister-in-law's face fell immediately.

'Nothing important, really. You know me, Rani, I'm not the one to complain about my daughter-in-law.'

'And you haven't ever. Why? Did Ruchi say something?'

Ruchi was Baban's wife.

'She hasn't and neither has anyone else,' her sister-in-law shook her head. 'I just don't want you to think of me as a typical mother-in-law. One of those who talk ill of their daughter-in-law every chance they get!'

'Boudi, don't I know you well enough?'

'It's not really about Ruchi. Her mother ...'

Rani was never very good at concealing her feelings.

'Oh! So Ruchi's mother is poking her nose in your business? she said, getting a tad excited. 'Trying to sway Baban? Is that so?'

'She's not really bothered about how I run things. She's more interested in Baban. Rani, she has got him totally under her thumb! He spends most of his days at their place and doesn't even bother coming home at night. If I say anything, he argues that Tollygunge is closer to his office. Plus, Ruchi is their only child so I must think of her parents as well. Can you imagine?'

'So let him spend a few days there every once in a while. What's the harm in that?' Rani put her hand on her sister-in-law's shoulder and said a little forcefully.

Her sister-in-law was lost in thought.

'Do you know what happened with Mejokaka?'

'No. What about them?'

'Mejokaka took great pains to raise Arnab, didn't he? Took all kinds of loans to send him to America. Got him married to a nice girl in Kolkata. This girl, Raktima, took her mother along with her to America. Arnab has refused to spend even a paisa to take Mejokaka for a visit, while on the other hand, he pays for his mother-in-law's flights to and from America. He says Raktima can't bear to live a day without her. She can't handle raising a child, going to the office, and looking after the home on her own. So, this one time, Mejokaka and Mejokaki paid for their own tickets to go to America. They came back within a month. It didn't feel like they were visiting their son but his mother-in-law!

'Mejokaki said Raktima's mother is a different creature now. The clothes she wears! Her hairstyle! She prattles off in English, drives cars, goes to parties thrown by other Bengalis! Arnab's friends are absolutely crazy about her. The woman drinks with her son-in-law's friends. Mejokaka and Mejokaki couldn't take it and ran away at the first chance. You don't know, Rani, even Ruchi's mother is trying to convince Baban to go abroad. Hong Kong, Singapore, London, the USA, wherever he can find a job. I have a feeling that Baban's life will pan out exactly like Arnab's!'

'The woman hangs out with Arnab's friends? Drinks with them?' Rani covered her mouth in surprise.

'Yes! Doesn't Mejokaki tell you anything? She has even said to her, "Mrs Roy, you're serving alcohol to Arnab's friends. It doesn't look right, does it?" And Mrs Roy said, "What kind of outdated talk is that? Arnab and I are like friends. No one gives a fuck about these formalities anymore, everyone's friends these days!"'

'Mother-in-law … friend …?'

'Yes!'

'Okay, now let's imagine the father-in-law drinking with his daughter-in-law's girlfriends. What then?'

'Why ask me, Rani?'

'Then the mother-in-law is a girlfriend and the father-in-law, the boyfriend?'

'What strange times we live in, Rani! Everyone's too comfortable with each other. There's no civility, no distance, no respect. Everyone's too keen to break all barriers and won't rest till everyone's treated the same! A pure heart, easy camaraderie, understanding each other, being respectful of other's feelings, opening yourself up to all kinds of people—this is what total strangers have come to expect from you! You're worthy of them only if you allow complete access to yourself. If you keep to yourself, don't wear your heart on your sleeve and maintain distance, others can't bear it. Perhaps it troubles them a lot. Why is everyone so averse to the word "conservative"? I think some traditions are good, aren't they?'

'Boudi, I can't think so deeply like you but all I can say is I can't allow or go along with my daughter-in-law referring to me as her friend!' Rani said. 'Isn't it appropriate to address one's mother-in-law as "Ma"? Shouldn't the closeness of the relationship be obvious if one addresses their father-in-law as "Baba"?

'I have one more reason to be upset!'

'What happened?'

'Baban's wife has shared a few photos of their family get-together on Facebook. In some of those photos, Baban's mother-in-law is hugging him from behind, kissing him on the cheeks. These photos ...!' Her voice choked up. 'Rani, I don't know if you are able to understand me. I'm not jealous. I know a mother-in-law is like your own mother; in fact, she is your mother, but isn't all this a bit too much? Why should the mother behave like this with her daughter's husband? Will it make the daughter happy to see them being so intimate? Or is she behaving like this because she always wanted a son of her own? Even I was desperate for a daughter but I don't behave like this, do I?'

'Why don't you tell Dada to hug Ruchi and kiss her the next time she visits? Tit for tat!'

'As if that will affect Baban in the least! By the looks of it, he doesn't mind being chummy with his parents-in-law either. Otherwise, he would have protested against it, wouldn't he?'

'God knows what has got into the mothers of girls. All of them want to move in with their daughter and son-in-law. Let the daughter and son-in-law live on their own! Why should they put up with nagging mothers-in-law? They'll have a nice life, won't have to slave away endlessly. But now, the mothers of girls want to be like cuckoos invading the crow's nest! The son-in-law should be raised by his parents, made into doctors and engineers, and all she'll do is marry her daughter to one of these guys, pack her off to her in-laws' for two days, and then bring both the daughter and son-in-law to her fold at the first chance she gets. A readymade son free of cost! She'll party with her son-in-law, drink with him, go to restaurants and only then will he be worthy of her. The sons take to the in-laws as close family while the parents become discarded goods. He's sick of looking at their faces, their voices grate on him, and that's why the in-laws are so much better. Nowadays, the parents of girls are very insecure! All of them have only one child and that's why it's so important to have the son-in-law under your thumb. No matter how independent a woman is, in some aspects, men are still more important, aren't they?'

'You know Arka, right? Baban's childhood friend,' her sister-in-law smiled ruefully. 'His mother and I are good friends. We've been friends since the time we would accompany our sons to school. Anyway, she called me one day and said, "Shampa, remember how we used to say we'd never speak ill of our daughters-in-law, we'd treat them like our daughters and we'd let them live their lives however they pleased? We promised we'd hand over our sons without any complaints and let the daughter-in-law take over the reins of the household. We used to say all this, remember? Oh, but my cursed fate! I do have a daughter-in-law but she's least interested in keeping a good home. She's left her heart behind at her parents' home. Whenever something catches her eye, she'll immediately buy it for her parents. Just the other day, she bought containers for her mother because the ones in their home are too old! But she knows nothing about what's going on in her mother-in-law's kitchen! She keeps two sarees and two nighties at her parents' home at all times. She comes and goes as she pleases and she doesn't really live here. She would rather go to her parents' home to dress up for a big event! Not only did I not get a daughter, but now my son feels like a stranger too. After returning from work, he brings out his car and takes his mother-in-law to Gariahat market to buy fish. What good did my big-heartedness do? My mother-in-law wouldn't get a good night's sleep without cursing me soundly and my daughter-in-law treats me like I don't matter at all! She keeps her distance like I'm her co-passenger on the metro!'

The teep from Rani's forehead had slipped off as she lay on the bed. She felt her forehead as she sat up straight. Her hands searched for it on the bedcover. It was nowhere to be found. Giving up, she fetched a box full of teep from her handbag and without looking at the mirror, stuck one in the space between her eyebrows.

'You have to leave now, right?' her sister-in-law sighed loudly and remarked.

'Yes, Boudi. It's time. But what are you thinking? What will you do about it?'

'I can't see them treating my son like a puppet, Rani! I hate it.'

'There's nothing you can do, Boudi. Both of us have a son each. We wouldn't feel like we had lost them if only we had daughters too. We would keep the son-in-law's mouth filled with sweets, treat them like princes, and treat them like our own sons. If it were possible, I wouldn't even bother to get my son married. God knows what's going to happen. I wonder if Bappa will even marry Razia ... But all I know is if he does end up marrying her, then the same fate awaits me. Her mother's voice and the way she looks don't sit right with me. I mean, she's a bit too modern, you know! Boudi, don't I look like an aunty?' Saying this, Rani posed like someone was waiting to take her photos.

'That's true! Like a real housewife,' her sister-in-law said and laughed. 'Won't you change? Is this what you will wear to Razia's?'

'No, not at all. I have brought a gorgeous saree. Handloom tussar. Wait, I'll show it to you. Boudi, tell me something—how do I reduce this tummy of mine? All that gymming did me no good. I have seen Razia's mother's photos on Facebook. My God, is she skinny! She was wearing black leggings and a black top and standing straight against a wall. Her hair was cut in layers. No one would say she's the same age as me! Razia had posted the photo and the caption said, "My mother rocks!" I'll look like a total grandma in front of her mother.'

'Rani, you are very beautiful and you no longer have to worry about running the household,' her sister-in-law answered. 'Your mother-in-law is dead. Bappa is doing well. He got a good job right after college. It's time to look after yourself, isn't it?'

'Lose some weight,' she winked and continued. 'Wear jeans and tops. I can't do all this in Baranagar but you should get a makeover!'

'Goodness!' Rani said. 'Before joining the women's association, all I did to dress up was plait my hair. I would be exhausted from running after Bappa all day. The entire day would be spent worrying about studies and exams. After Bappa was done with his school-leaving examinations, I looked at the other women in the association and changed my style. I got a haircut, dyed my hair, started to wear only boutique sarees, put a big teep on my forehead, wore oxidised jewellery. Everyone was crazy about my tussar silks! I would only wear kalamkari blouses. But now it turns out that young women don't dress like this anymore. Only fatsos like me do! Flowers in our hair, teep as wide as saucers! Slim women who care about their figure don't bother to dress so loud. All they do is put on a pair of jeggings, a top, fasten their hair with a clip, and that's it! You'd think they had just got out of bed. Superb confidence! And why not? The secret is in their glowing health!' Rani exhaled loudly.

'Bouma, the boris on the terrace ...' her mother woke up from her nap and said rubbing her eyes. She then lost her train of thought.

'Oh, I had completely forgotten that Rani is here. I've been thinking in my sleep, who is it that's chatting away! I'm getting old!' she said.

'Thank God, you haven't forgotten who I am,' teased Rani.

'What kind of talk is that! It's you who doesn't visit me anymore.'

'And thank God for that! If you were like the mothers of today and kept crying for your daughter all day, then perhaps I'd not have been able to take care of my home diligently. But those days are long gone. These days, the girls get impatient as soon as they reach marriageable age. They get hold of a groom anyhow. I have the same thing to say about the boys too. After all, this is how it has always been. You have to live your life, your parents won't coddle you forever.'

Rani went into her sister-in-law's room to get dressed. Her brother had joined a private firm after retirement. It would be nine o'clock before he returned.

'Is your daughter-in-law coming home today?' Rani asked her sister-in-law before she left.

'Who knows if my son will come home today! Let alone his wife.'

Rani was quite surprised to see Razia's home. They lived in a huge flat on the twelfth floor. The house was elegantly decorated. They had money, taste too. 'Come, I'll show you around,' Razia said.

The common area opened into a big balcony. Razia's mother's name was Smita.

'I love balconies,' she said. 'That's why I have designed it according to my taste.'

And she had, indeed. The floor was lined with black and white tiles and there were dark green iron benches in two corners of the balcony. Right next to each bench stood a lamp post. Another side of the wall was painted with a colourful mural. A round coffee table stood in the middle. Every corner was covered with plants. Rani was friends with many wealthy women but none of them had such a beautiful balcony. Taking in the sights, she decided it was time to tell her husband to renovate their house. Their son would get married any day now. It was as good a time as any to make the house brand new again.

She knew she would let Bappa and his wife keep the third floor to themselves. It had been renovated with modern fittings. There were many rooms on that floor. One of them could be easily converted into a balcony. The black and white tiles were so unique! Though, of course, they could not do the same. That would be copying Razia's mother. Instead, Rani would ask for a floor of black granite. She looked at Smita once more. She was wearing a white skirt and a skintight blue top. The slippers on her feet were something else too! Silver and studded with sparkling faux gems.

'My mother only shops in Bangkok. She and her sister are always going on shopping trips!' Razia had once told Rani. Rani, on the other hand, had never stepped out of Kolkata without her husband, Shekhar.

Razia's father was the proud owner of an independent business. She had completed a master's degree in English and had recently joined her father in the family business. Shekhar had his own business too, but Bappa had studied engineering and was working in Sector V in Salt Lake City. Shekhar was not too keen for Bappa to join him in the business. The government was very corrupt, bribery was an everyday affair and it was impossible to do anything without plying the contractors with alcohol and women. Shekhar had no interest in his son being a part of this filth. In fact, he'd have been happier if he had had a daughter instead. Rani, of course, hadn't told anyone about this.

'Rani, I haven't slept with anyone except you,' Shekhar had told her. 'But someday I will tell you how much I have spent on call girls! Yuck!'

She couldn't blame Shekhar. That was just how the system was. On one hand, Shekhar was paying whores to keep his contractors happy while on the other hand, Rani had been made the president of the local women's association and was raising funds for making women financially independent.

'Do you like looking after the business?' she asked Razia.

'I love it, Aunty. I'm born to rule! I was not meant to work in a nine-to-five job,' she answered with a smile. Razia, youthful-looking and wearing a dress, could be mistaken for an eighth-grade student.

Born to rule! Rani's face fell. By now, she knew there was no choice but to hand over Bappa to Razia's family when the time came. The mother and daughter behaved like sisters. She couldn't keep her depressing thoughts at bay. If she were to be entirely truthful, then the mother was more attractive than the daughter. She knew how young men these days had a thing for older women. In fact, someone was telling her just the other day that young men were so insecure about being in a relationship that they preferred to be with older, married women. Rani decided she'd go through Ruchi's profile once she was home. To check what she was posting. She had to see what it would look like if Baban's mother-in-law hugged him and kissed him. Rani was already bubbling with anger. One, she was infuriated with how she looked. Shapeless and clumsy. Second, she was annoyed with Bappa. It was already seven and yet, he was nowhere to be seen. Shekhar must be on his way home now. She rang Bappa while chatting with Smita.

'I'm almost there,' he said and hung up right after.

'Oh, you called Bappa?' said Razia.

As soon as he walked in through the door, Bappa flung his jacket on the sofa in a way that confirmed he was a regular at Razia's home. They had already drunk tea once. Pushpa, the maid, got coffee for Bappa.

'Not coffee,' he said. 'I want tea with ginger today. My throat feels scratchy. Looks like I have a cold coming on.'

Rani could not take her eyes off her son. He had not even hinted to his mother that he was already so much at home at Razia's place! Didn't he tell her only yesterday that going out with her did not mean that they were ready to marry just yet? Or was it because of his two failed relationships that he was actually desperate to get married quickly and was only pretending to be indifferent about it?

She felt bad. The youth these days do not have it easy. Her parents had arranged her marriage and she had been with the same man ever since. She was given no chance to judge for herself if she liked being married to or living with him. Before she knew it, she was spending sleepless nights worrying about Bappa's future. There was no time to enjoy the present; the years had hurtled towards the future. She was preoccupied with this life and there was no escape from it. But it was different for the new generation. They were constantly thinking whether being together was worth it.

A torrent of thoughts washed over her but she did not stop chattering with Smita and Razia.

'You're coming to the picnic with us, aren't you?' Razia asked Bappa suddenly.

'I can't wake up so early, Razia. I have had a busy week. I'll sleep till noon tomorrow.'

'Tell him to come, please, please,' Razia pouted and said to Rani.

Rani did Razia's bidding but Bappa refused to change his mind. She did not know why but Bappa's stubbornness filled her with great joy.

'What's this picnic? Where is it?' asked Rani.

'My sister and her husband live in America. I mean, their home is in Kolkata but they've been living with their daughter who is married and lives there. So, you could say they've settled there,' explained Smita. 'But they travel to India every six months. They are here now and whenever they visit, they arrange picnics and throw parties.'

'What about the son-in-law's parents?' Rani asked.

'They live somewhere around Sonarpur.'

'Doesn't your niece ask her in-laws to come too?'

'No, I don't think so,' Smita answered nonchalantly. 'At least, I don't know anything about it.'

'These days, men seem to prefer to live with their in-laws. One of my friend's daughters got married in Delhi. Her parents moved in with her right after. My friend and her husband wrapped up their lives here and moved to Delhi for good. Meanwhile, the son-in-law's mother became terribly lonely after her husband died. But she has not left her home in Behala. What a pitiful life she has now! She admits herself to the hospital when she feels unwell. She's not a unique case; this is the story of every home. The daughter-in-law has shifted her mother to Bangalore with her for her cancer treatment while the husband's mother suffers from osteoarthritis. There's no one to look after her. That's why perhaps our sons ...'

Rani threw a sharp look in her son's direction. She could not say for sure if he was listening to her. He seemed to be busy on his phone. Did Razia and her mother gauge the deep hurt in her voice? Perhaps not.

'No matter what anyone says, women are responsible for their homes. The men consider themselves passersby,' Razia said. 'For instance, see what goes on in our home. My father is the earning member; everything is paid for with the money he makes, but you won't believe how guilty he feels when he breaks a glass. He can't stop saying sorry to Ma. You'd think he's a complete outsider.

'And these days, most women are working too. You can imagine what their lives are like, especially if they are mothers too—it's pathetic! It's much easier to have your mother around instead of your mother-in-law. You can do whatever you want, the differences aren't as many. They don't feel guilty asking their mothers to make them a cup of tea, or look after the baby, or give them a head massage. You're still free. And because men think of themselves as guests in their own homes, it doesn't bother them if they have to live with their in-laws. In fact, a mother and daughter won't fight so he's at peace too. Moreover, even kids suffer when the daughter-in-law and mother-in-law bicker with each other. But that isn't the case here. The couple can fly off for a holiday whenever they feel like, the wife's mother will take care of the children.

'No matter what anyone says, even today, the maternal grandmother is more protective than the paternal one. In the same way, a maternal uncle is closer than a paternal uncle. People have finally understood what arrangement works better for them. The social structure is changing. The mother of the wife is more precious than the husband's mother! I mean, she's more in demand. From a sociological point of view, for ages, women have been kept in check through the institution called the family. If the daughter lets her mother have a say in her life, then the mother feels comfort in knowing that she's still important to her daughter. To them, this involvement means respect, gratitude, repaying a debt, but that's bullshit! It's still a give-and-take relationship. Even the girl's parents know very well that they have no one but her to look after them in their old age.'

Razia smiled knowingly after finishing her monologue. Smita did not look particularly affected by her daughter's opinions, as though she had listened to them many times before.

'Your father was never comfortable around my mother. He is still very formal with her,' she said.

'He's from an earlier generation, Ma. It was different for them,' said Razia.

'Apparently, my grandmother has always kept her head covered before my father and neither has she looked him directly in his eyes,' Smita turned to Rani and said. 'Can you imagine?'

Rani did not know what to say to Razia. Moreover, what she had said was completely true. For a multitasking woman, a mother was a more useful presence than a mother-in-law. She thought about how the mothers slaved away on their daughters' behalf. Since that was the case, wasn't it better to be the son's mother? She could at least enjoy a degree of freedom even if it meant being shipped off to an old-age home. Travel, eat to your heart's content, take a nap whenever you want to. All that was much better than raising a child! She'd have to explain the situation to her sister-in-law exactly in the manner that Razia had.

'O Boudi, don't get into all that trouble. Let Ruchi visit you every few months. It's better that way. The closer she pulls you in, the more you should be prepared to raise her babies!'

The two families met with each other, talked amongst themselves, and now it was time for Rani to leave.

'I wanted to say something if you don't mind,' seizing the moment, Smita said. 'Bappa returns late from work on some nights and my daughter would rather party with her friends at home on the weekend. I hope you won't mind if Bappa stays over on some nights because of all this. We used to be strangers once but not anymore. That's why I can be so honest with you, Rani!'

Rani felt her insides burn with this terrible insult. Not only had they called her to show off their home and their wealth but now they also wanted to stake claims on her son. Was that why she had been invited in the first place? Just to ask her for permission? She was Bappa's mother and Shekhar was his father. Were they entirely disposable? Had Bappa truly lost his mind to this two-bit girl, her company and sex? Why did he have to stay the night? Couldn't he at least wait till marriage? What was the need to stay over at Razia's place before that? What should she say? Should she still pretend to be civil?

'No, I can't grant him permission,' she answered. 'I won't allow it. He can party all he wants to but he must drive back home at night. Why should he stay over at his girlfriend's? Also, we don't really know each other. You should visit us at home too. Razia, plan a date soon. Let's go, Bappa,' she said.

'Ma, why didn't you give permission?' Bappa said to Rani when the two of them were alone. 'Ridiculous! Why did you get into a foul mood? What the hell happened? Why did you get so angry?'

'Do you want to marry her? In that case, marry her as soon as you can. What's the need to prolong it? Marry her and live with them. Visit me when you can.'

'Why should I live with them? Bappa narrowed his eyes and asked. 'Don't I have my own house?'

'Who knows, Bappa? I don't know anything anymore. Now I know that their house is far bigger and much prettier than ours. Didn't you always complain about all the grilles on our windows? You said that our house looked like a jail. In contrast, there's so much open space in Razia's house.'

'Ma, we live in a house. They live in a flat. Baba can easily buy a similar flat if he wants to.'

Tears streamed down Rani's face.

'And what if he couldn't? Would you leave us then, Bappa? Tell me the truth. You can't stand your Ma and Baba anymore, right? They are so boring!'

'Ma, just glancing at your face brings me so much peace. How can you even say these things? I don't want to leave you and that's why I'm still in Kolkata. The office wants me to work on a project in the US. But I have refused it. Why? You are wrong, Ma. You are hurting yourself. I have already spoken to Razia. I have told her I love my parents and I intend to live with them. It's true that she's her parents' only child and is responsible for their well-being. We'll manage everything. Don't worry so much.' Bappa put an arm round his mother as he spoke to her.

Rani's life was no longer the same. She was very confused. First, she signed up for classes at the World Yoga Society. Next, she put herself on a strict no-carb diet. A ridiculous amount of money was spent on new outfits and cosmetics. She had convinced herself that she had to compete with Razia's mother. Still, no matter how hard she tried or how well she dressed, she could not outshine Razia's mother in the looks department. This led to her cooking furiously at home all around the clock. She went out of her way to make strange new recipes. Bappa was fed these new creations, which in turn resulted in him gaining an unnatural amount of weight.

'Ma, enough. Stop now, please,' he said with folded hands.

In the meantime, Razia visited their house with her parents. Shekhar quickly became friends with Razia's father while Rani could not relax around Razia's mother. She would look at Razia and think to herself how she could not muster up any maternal feelings for her. And she wouldn't ever! She could only think of her as a co-passenger on the Darjeeling Mail. She did not look away from Smita even for a moment and was obsessed with everything she did and said. After all, Rani had to know how seriously Smita was trying to influence Bappa. When Razia asked everyone to gather on the sofa for a photo, Rani had to shut her eyes when she saw Bappa settling down next to Smita. Neither the would-be son-in-law nor the mother-in-law cared about the boundaries of their relationship. Smita threw herself on her would-be son-in-law as she embraced him for a photo.

'I haven't clicked photos with Bappa in a long time. Will you click one?' Rani said to Razia while they were taking photographs.

'What's the need for that!' Bappa remarked and tried to slink away.

'I don't have a photo with you, Bappa,' Rani said.

She posed with her son and Razia continued to take the photos. She suspected that everyone's mouths were open wide in surprise. Shekhar looked on, as did Razia's father, Smita too, and even Razia as she clicked away on the camera. Rani puckered her lips and loudly kissed Bappa's face. It was like she had transformed into a young mother and Bappa was in the second standard and all the tiredness of her years had been wiped away. The long years of taking him to school in the heat, rain and cold had made her weary to the bone but now, all of a sudden, she was no longer exhausted.

The next day, Bappa returned home with a heavy heart.

'Ma, Razia and I have broken up,' he said to Rani. 'She, or rather they, thinks that you are obsessed with me. You are mentally ill. You have lost it even though I'm not married yet. And when I do get married, you won't let Razia and me live in peace. They said you need help.'

'Is that why she left you?'

'Razia didn't want to but she said the relationship should just be about the two of us. She doesn't want to see you anymore. Why, Ma? Why did you behave like that? Even the other day, you were going on and on about being the son's mother. And yesterday—'

'What about yesterday, Bappa?'

'Let it be. Do you understand what I'm trying to tell you? Mothers have no role to play in the life of a man my age.'

Rani could not take it anymore. She started to bawl.

'But a girl becomes closer to her mother at this age. She realises the importance of her mother, isn't that so?'

'You don't want Razia and me to be together,' Bappa said sharply. 'You're jealous of her mother. For shame!'

'No, no, no, not at all,' Rani said between her sobs.

Calming down after a few days, Rani realised that she hadn't done anything that would force Razia and her to be estranged forever. It wasn't that she was a regular visitor before. After marriage, she'd probably visit her once in a while and stay no longer than fifteen days. Let her not come to their place if she didn't want to. Rani called her sister-in-law and told her everything.

'Everyone's obsessed with their children. So why am I being blamed for it?'

'Don't you get it?' her sister-in-law said. 'They are very conservative, too. A lot has happened here, by the way. A family in our neighbourhood is going through hell. A couple died in a car accident and their ten-year-old daughter has become an orphan. Her uncle lives in Nagpur and he didn't bother to visit even in these horrific circumstances. Your brother and I have adopted her. The neighbours are happy about it. The girl's name is Mampi. Baban and Ruchi were vehemently against us adopting her legally. But nothing deterred us. We had a terrible fight and the two have left home for good. I won't change my mind. I will bring Mampi over on Poila Boishakh. It's an auspicious day. You must visit us then. Promise me you will.'

'Boudi, a ten-year-old kid?' said Rani, shocked. 'Will you be able to raise her? Isn't it a lot of trouble? The hassle of schools, tuition and an education!'

'Of course, I will. Just you see. There are only a few days to go. I can't wait any longer. You already know how desperate I have been for a daughter. You have to come home.'

Rani detected a youthful candour in her sister-in-law's voice.

'I will,' she said.

A HAPPY COUPLE

After leaving office, Sutirtha called Ahana and said, 'On my way. The traffic is hopeless. It'll be at least eight o'clock before I reach.'

'You're already on the bus?' Ahana asked.

'No. Partha asked me to wait for two minutes. I will have a smoke with him. Then we'll go for tea at Prasad's stall. I'll take the bus after that,' Sutirtha said.

There were many buses that went from New Town to Rajarhat, then Narkeldanga and finally, all the way to College Street. The bus stand was right in front of the office. It would take Sutirtha about an hour to reach home if he took the bus from Karunamoyee to Ultadanga. He would get off at Amherst Street, walk for a few minutes, and Mullick Nibas would appear to his left. The house was built in 1880 by his grandfather's father's eldest brother. It was inherited by his single child, a daughter. Therefore, everyone who had lived in Mullick Nibas in the last hundred years was not a Mullick. Most of them were Mitters. Sutirtha's grandfather's father started a press on the first floor of the house at the turn of the previous century. The business soon went bankrupt and he sank into debt. He was not only forced to pack up the press but also let the first floor out on rent. The press made way for a hosiery factory but that didn't survive for long either. At present, the first floor served as a storehouse for a well-known saree shop on College Street. Furthermore, another room had also been sublet as an office for a new publisher.

The house was divided equally between Sutirtha and his aunt, Juthika. The first floor belonged to his aunt. Sutirtha did not know the exact details of the arrangements she had with her boarders, including the amount she collected in rent. All he knew was his aunt's son, whom he called Babu-da, had wanted to rent out one of the rooms on the terrace. However, Ahana's disapproval made him promptly install a collapsible gate on the stairs leading from the first floor to the second. Not just the gate, he also enclosed their side of the verandah with iron grilles. Sutirtha was not affluent and Ahana had sold her jewellery to install such security measures in their part of the house. Since then, Sutirtha has been totally cut off from his aunt's family. He did not have any other relatives.

Ahana was the only daughter of her parents and she did not have a big family to boast of either. She did not work at an office nor was she in touch with any of her friends. Sutirtha earned a pittance. Having friends also meant additional expenses. They did not have the money for it. Therefore, Ahana kept herself confined at home, and Sutirtha divided his time between the office and adda at Mrityunjay's place. This was how they had wasted many years.

Besides going to the cinema once in a while, Ahana would go to different fairs all year round. Walking around the fair, looking at the displays, and coming home without buying anything was particularly enjoyable to the couple. These days, everyone seemed to have a lot of money to squander. While Kolkata's economic growth had remained elusive to the naked eye, it was true that the people of the city had more money than ever before. They spent a lot on unnecessary things! Sutirtha would like to know where all that money came from. He had no money to spare and therefore, the material markers of belonging to the twenty-first century, of living in 2016, were missing from his life. He had recently taken to Facebook while his wife was already addicted to it. Apart from that, everything else in his life was dated. If Sutirtha hid his smartphone from view, stood in any corner of his home on a Sunday afternoon and took a good look at his surroundings, he would find himself transported twenty years back in time. His world was trapped in the cobwebs of his days. The same old clothesline and cotton towels, the same old Ahana in her same old salwar kameez that cost no more than four hundred rupees at the Hatibagan market. The same old way in which she tucked her dupattas on the iron railings ...

Even the pots and pans in the kitchen, barring a teacup or two, had stayed the same over the years. Rice was still cooked in the same battered pot that his mother used. Fine lines had appeared on the red floor with black borders but no repairs had been undertaken. Damp patches, which he imagined looked like Karl Marx's face, had appeared on the bathroom wall when Sutirtha was a schoolboy. Over the years, Marx's stubble had grown into a luscious beard.

A religious ceremony had been conducted in the house at some point in Sutirtha's childhood. He still remembered who had attended, the taste of the shinni, the loud ululations and the sound when the conch was blown. The event had been memorialised in the still visible, faint lines of the swastika design his mother had drawn on the floor all those years ago. The room had belonged to her. Even today, Sutirtha never bought more than a quarter of a kilo of sugar from the neighbourhood grocery shop. He had never shopped at an air-conditioned supermarket. There was no LED TV at home. Ahana had purchased a second-hand AC but neither had ever felt hot enough to turn it on.

This was the general picture of Sutirtha's life. They had eaten ilish only once this year. Ahana had eagerly posted photos on Facebook. He'd never forget that day. Fried ilish, ilish curry, steamed ilish and ilish head with pui shaak leaves had been cooked. Before long, the photos had one hundred and fifty likes and nearly forty comments. All before they had even eaten this fish.

'I shouldn't have posted the photos,' Ahana, whose face had puffed up and turned red after all that cooking, said to him.

'Why not?' Sutirtha asked naïvely.

'What will everyone think if we post photos on only one day? They'll figure out we don't eat ilish on other days.'

'Who's keeping count …'

'Everyone. You don't know anything. You have no idea what Facebook is like.'

'Why wouldn't I? Of course I do.'

'It's something else. It's a whole different world out there and they are all waiting quietly to pounce on you and tear you to shreds. To prey on your weaknesses and destroy your integrity.'

'In that case, it's better to stay off it.'

Ahana was quiet for a while.

'But Facebook has given me a new lease of life,' she said. 'I'll disappear from people's lives if I delete my account. I almost didn't exist before Facebook. What was the point of my staying alive? Do you remember that day when you said I looked like a Bikash Bhattacharjee painting? I was standing against the window of Ma's bedroom and my hands were holding the latch as I stared into the distance as the light of the setting sun fell on my face. I immediately asked you to take a photo on your phone. I posted it on Facebook and received so much appreciation, so many likes and comments. So many people wanted to be my friend. An illustrator quickly painted the image in watercolour to go with a famous writer's story. I found out about this from Facebook too. There was so much excitement! Many accused him of plagiarism. They wanted me to report him to the magazine's editor. Someone said there was no need to add more fuel to the fire. Artists were known to take inspiration from photographs. I have stood by this window for many years. The sunlight always fell on my face in this exact manner. And yet, the image was lost somewhere in the folds of your insignificant life and entirely ignored by you. To you, it was an ordinary occurrence. But thanks to Facebook, I realised that this ordinary moment was worthy of so much praise and adulation.'

Ahana paused for breath.

'Someone commented that the window slats were beautiful,' she continued, smiling contentedly. 'Had anyone spared a look at these windows before? This one moment of sunlight falling on my face now exists in eternity and has been seen by people everywhere in the world. There's a photo my father had taken of my mother at the Puri beach. My mother is standing in the water as the waves lash against her. It's a lovely photo but it has not travelled outside the red-coloured photo album. Other than them, only I had seen the photo. My aunt had seen it too. Once, I had shown the photo to my school friends and their mothers when they had come over. That's all. My mother's life was ordinary and no one had really bothered to open the album to look at her photos. My life is as unremarkable as hers. Still, that one single moment put so many people in my orbit. We never had any provision for such excitement in our lives, did we? No, no, I absolutely cannot live without Facebook!'

Sutirtha had never thought so seriously about social media. He barely posted any photos. He was an introvert. He also refrained from expressing his views on politics. He'd take the bus at the end of the day and if he was lucky enough to get a seat, he'd settle into it comfortably before logging into his Facebook account. Then, no matter how bad the traffic, how crowded the bus, how hot, or how unbearable the stench of the sweating bodies packed close together, they did not bother him in the least. He would plug his ears with earphones and immediately forget that he was Sutirtha Mitter, an ordinary maintenance worker at an office. The intolerable pollution, the forty-three-degree heat wave, the blaring horns, the monotony of the commute, none of these affected him. As far as he was concerned, this was Facebook's greatest boon.

Ahana transferred the ilish dishes to a different set of bowls and took another round of photos.

'Keeping them in stock,' she said. 'I will post these photos after two weeks. My Facebook friends will be impressed to see that I'm having ilish twice in a month!' Sutirtha's initial look of surprise gave way to frank admiration.

'That's the only way to stay relevant,' Ahana said. 'It's not so easy. So what if Facebook is the new world order? It's still an order alright. The fact that it is a virtual community doesn't change anything!'

Ahana was proven right. She posted the rest of the photos ten days later.

'Ahana, has your husband got a promotion? There's always ilish in your kitchen,' said the first comment under the post.

'Looks like you'll eat every ilish in the market!' someone else said.

'You are an expert cook, Didi,' commented a young woman. 'That's why your husband brings ilish from the market every other day.'

Did the young woman really think Ahana was an expert cook? People on Facebook were prone to exaggeration.

'Do you see now? Wasn't I right?' Ahana gloated to Sutirtha. She was smart. She posted a common reply to all comments.

'I won't play along if you tease me like this! I won't show you how I have cooked the ilish. I'm scared you guys will order an IT raid on me!'

As usual, Sutirtha found a window seat on the bus. He logged into Facebook.

'Dad, I love you so much. Happy birthday to you, our dearest Dad.' It was accompanied by a photo of the dearest dad with his three children. It was a post from his colleague Nimai Mukherjee's daughter, Arpita.

Nimai Mukerjee was a sharp one. He was second only to the manager in the maintenance department at Union Space. He had an incredible memory. He knew exactly which lamp had burst in the lobby of a particular floor and where the door to a toilet cubicle was unhinged. He did not need the register. He could easily recall who was sent on inspection and who for repair. His salary was no more than thirty thousand rupees but his daughter addressed him as 'Dad'. Could you believe it! He wore modest trousers and shirts made by the neighbourhood tailor. He did not wear a belt but always wore his ancient HMT watch. This Nimai was Dad to his children! This was possible only in the age of Facebook.

Sutirtha had once been to Nimai-da's house. He was wearing a lungi and was busy cleaning the drains.

'Can't just spend all my time looking after the office, can I? I have to maintain my own house too!' he told Sutirtha.

The next post on his feed was Ahana's. It had been uploaded fifteen minutes ago.

'Homemade egg chicken rolls! My hubby's favourite. He says it's even better than Nizam's! Trust me—they are!'

Two photos accompanied the text. They were taken from different angles. Sutirtha was surprised. What all did she even get up to these days! In this filtered version, they were no longer a poor couple. Their lives appeared so cushy. They seemed perfectly happy together. As happy as those in TV commercials, with a lifestyle to flaunt. And what about him? Why, he was a hubby now. Like he had a white-collar job. A corporate executive! He kept busy all day. No time to spare for the missus. Couldn't go to sleep without downing two pegs of whisky. Seeing his wife's Facebook posts made him feel worthless.

Ahana had served the egg chicken rolls on an ancient German silver platter. The red tablecloth was actually a bedspread. Sutirtha knew this. There was a bone china glass that belonged to his mother and Ahana had put a stem of bougainvillaea in it. Nothing else was in the frame. Nothing else of the dilapidated house was captured in this shot. And along with this, a caption written in English. He was hubby and Nimai-da, Dad.

This was the language that ruled the world. Even gibberish in English sounded like high literature. Sutirtha and Ahana's way of life, their financial status, the furniture and decor of their house, none of that fit this language. However, no one could fault Sutirtha or Ahana for using it. No one could accuse them of being unsuited to it. And that, exactly, was the joy of Facebook.

Ahana was careful and did not post photos that showed their clothesline or the towels hanging on them. Or photos of herself wearing nighties, or of her grimy kitchen and the tattered pillowcases on their bed. However, there were many who did. They forgot that Facebook was a world in itself. They gladly exposed parts of themselves that should have been hidden. Black, greasy, nausea-inducing korai overflowing with unappetising-looking chicken curry. 'My special boneless chicken curry. Yummy!'

They dressed up prettily for their selfies, but behind them was a dirty, unkempt house. The pillow spilling out of its case, the wide-open bathroom door with the toilet in view. Still, Sutirtha was scared. He worried the truth would be out in the open one of these days. Soon, everyone would know that the elastic band of his underwear had come loose.

'No one invites us. What should we do?' Ahana said when he returned home. 'Everyone goes out all the time and they post photos too. I can't do anything about it. Everyone posts photos of eating in restaurants. Can't we?'

She then went to the terrace and spent a long time there.

'Tomorrow I'll post a photo of a wedding,' she declared after she was back.

Sutirtha looked up in surprise. 'I'll wear a Banarasi saree tomorrow and post a photo,' Ahana said, smiling conspiratorially.

'Your posts are fine, Ahana. The owl that you spotted on the neem tree, the karabi flowers in their pots, the full moon, the fairs and the Vidyasagar Setu from Outram Ghat. Why do you want to post about your personal life?'

'Do you know people even post photos of their report cards? They go out to eat at restaurants and post photos of the bill. What's wrong with it? Our lives are so inconsequential anyway. What's wrong with a few people knowing how I live?'

Sutirtha left for his nightly adda without taking his phone along.

'We're attending a wedding tomorrow. Don't forget,' Ahana said after him.

He did not turn around. Mrityunjay's wife was addicted to Facebook too. She would surely ask them the details of the wedding if she saw Ahana's photos. What would Sutirtha say then? Which lucky couple's wedding did they attend? Mrityunjay's wife was on good terms with many people from Sutirtha's family. He would have to be careful. Perhaps he could say it was someone from Ahana's family. He started walking at a frantic speed. Facebook was a world in itself. Sutirtha was desperate to exile himself from it.

PICTURE PERFECT

Gopa was fast asleep. It had rained two days in a row and the heat had dissipated. There were five windows in the room and each of them was as big as a door. The house was built in 1890 and designed by a British architect. Bappa had installed two air conditioners of two tonnes each in her room. It didn't cool otherwise. However, it made Gopa extremely uncomfortable to turn on both air conditioners and snore away as the metre ratcheted up an obnoxiously expensive electricity bill. The wet air after a heavy rainfall soothed the oppressive heat. She threw open all the windows and covered herself with a thin sheet, like she was used to, as she took a siesta after lunch. No, she didn't go to sleep right away.

She parted her curtains just so to sneak a quick look into Pinky's room. The mother and son duo were snoring away happily. These days, Bublai did not sleep very well. He'd wake up even if you tiptoed into the room on. And then he'd stare you down with angry eyes. He was just two months old. There was no one else in Pinky and Paramesh's two-member family in Mumbai who would look after the young mother and the newborn. Gopa was ready to travel the distance. Bappa had already booked her ticket. Then all of a sudden, Paramesh's company wanted him to be in Dubai for the next six months. The couple decided that in the meantime, Pinky would move in with her mother in Kolkata. She would visit her in-laws once in Belur. Since Pinky's mother-in-law was missing from the scene, Gopa did not mind her daughter visiting her in-laws. The couple had decided what the next few would look like and Gopa had no objections.

'Ma, you don't have a problem with this arrangement, do you?' Pinky asked.

'Why? I'm always at home,' she answered immediately. 'The farthest I go anywhere is your house. I'll be relieved if you're in Kolkata and I won't have to travel all the way to Mumbai. I don't like that city at all! I miss Kolkata so much when I'm there. I hate it when I can't go around as I please. I worry I will lose my voice if I don't get to see Kajal and Binati at least once a week. Come as soon as you can. It's for the best.'

Thanks to Bublai, everyone spoke in whispers around the house. Pinky claimed her baby could already recognise the sound of her breathing and other people's breath sent him into a tizzy. Unbelievable! Gopa looked fondly at the excited new mother and experienced a rush of affection for her. She could not recognise her daughter at times.

She took a quick look at her grandson before coming into her room. She drifted into a deep sleep as soon as she lay on the bed. Even today, she enjoyed her siesta very much. It was her weakness, if you will. Mala truly was a darling. She'd bring a cup, teapot, biscuits, chanachur and cake (if there was any) on a tray and gently wake her up. Oh, how she enjoyed sipping on her tea while sleep still clung to her eyelids! Juhi had trained Mala very well. How well she looked after Gopa!

And now, Pinky too. Juhi had added Shankari to the domestic staff after Pinky's arrival. She looked after Bublai. The sturdy and well-built Shankari was the right person to look after a newborn.

Still asleep, she rattled off a series of questions when she felt Mala's touch on her skin. 'Brought tea? What's the time? Is it dark outside or just cloudy?'

'Cloudy. I haven't brought the tea. Get up, Mashi. Look who's here. Your other grandson. Your son's son.'

Gopa woke up with a start. 'Where? Riju is here? Where is he?' She could hear Bublai crying in the distance. 'Has he come with his mother?'

'Yes!' Mala's face lit up with a smile. 'Shall I make tea for them?'

'Does Riju drink tea?'

'Only for Boudi then.'

Gopa could not help but feel happy to see how pleased Mala was about Riju's visit. She addressed Pritha as 'Boudi'. Juhi would fire her if she got to know about it. Or perhaps she was just overthinking it. Maybe Juhi didn't care how the domestic staff addressed their employers. Who knows! It was impossible to know the inner workings of someone's mind. Wasn't it strange how we sometimes fixated on inconsequential things? Moreover, Gopa did not know Juhi all that well. She had never stayed in this house.

'Should I quickly change my saree?'

'Why, what's wrong with it? Have your in-laws come for a visit?'

'Alright, alright. Quickly turn on the lights. The ones in the verandah too. Pinky's room—'

Mala switched on the lights and darted out of the room before Gopa could finish. She climbed out of bed and examined herself in the wardrobe mirror. She fixed her saree, ran her fingers through her hair, and put her glasses back on before making her way to the other room. She had never felt this before, but today she suspected the windows, doors and curtains looked rather dirty. Juhi had ordered a new set of curtains for the house around a year ago. The house was crowded with maids, the washing machine was state-of-the-art and yet, how dirty the curtains looked! Why should there be even a speck of dirt on them? Disgusting.

'Where's he? Where's my Dadubhai?' she called out while entering the room. She did not know what or who would turn up. She had never been so confused in her life.

Pritha was there. Riju too. A one-year-old baby was playing with a teddy bear on Pinky's bed. He looked like a ruddy-cheeked white man's baby. Gopa's head spun for a moment. She did not know Pritha had had a baby! She had come to this house after two years. But why all of a sudden? What was the reason? Then again, even the last time too she had turned up unannounced.

She couldn't process so much in one go. After all, she was getting on in age. She had just turned sixty-seven. Still, she felt eternally restless. Every single thing seemed to demand her attention. It only took her a moment to become anxious. There was a reason why she asked Mala to switch on every light in the house. The houses in north Kolkata were poorly lit. Some rooms in the house were still fitted with colourful chandeliers though Gopa had never seen them lit in her own lifetime. She had not taken any initiative to light them either.

The chandeliers were shrouded in dust. Those who lived in north Kolkata were misers. This was absolutely true. Pritha could not stand poorly lit spaces. 'Should I buy some high voltage bulbs?' she said the very next day after moving in.

For a brief moment, Gopa was reminded of those days when Prita lived in the same house as her. Both Bappa and Pritha. The biggest, most airy room with the en-suite bathroom was given to the newlywed couple. The windows were covered with lace-trimmed curtains and dark blue drapes. Pritha had furnished the room according to her liking before they were even married. The room, even now, was exactly how she had left it.

The memories of the past, both near and distant, tugged at her heart. And there was also the reality of the present. She realised there were things she did not know, could not know and did not need to know. She arranged her face to show just the right amount of excitement and anxiety.

'Oh my, isn't that my Riju! Dadubhai, my darling!' she exclaimed, opened her arms and drew her grandson into them.

'How are you?' Riju asked in a faint voice, his head lowered. He sounded helpless and very vulnerable.

Oh, why did Gopa think that? There was no reason to. Pritha was a good mother to Riju. He studied at La Martiniere and took music lessons too. Gopa knew this. She was seeing Riju after two years. Bappa's only son. Her grandson. The son of her son. He looked exactly like Bappa at that age. Oh, what a shy little kid! He had a broad forehead and a long nose. She remembered how back in the day, old men and women would scrutinise a child's features, read their faces and reveal what destiny had in store for them. She could not exactly call herself modern but gone were the days when these things were taken seriously. These superstitions were lost with time. Not once had she felt like a grandmother, especially in the way she knew them to be. Her mind turned to the memories of her own grandmother.

Riju's cool eyes, broad forehead and strong jaw pointed to a well-educated, intelligent demeanour. A good sign! He would be lucky to be as sharp as his father. Just like him, he would do great things in life too. How was he at school, anyway? How embarrassing that Gopa knew nothing about it.

Riju turned ten this year. Or was it eleven? Gopa did not know what came over but she could barely manage to speak as she held Riju to her breast. She could not convey any emotions at all. She could not coddle him or slather him with kisses. Her eyes did not moisten; in fact, they felt unnaturally dry. She did not know what had come over her. She shied away from being too honest around Pritha.

'What good are my tears to her, anyway? What's the point of baring my heart?' she thought to herself.

She cried for Riju every once in a while, but only in complete privacy. She did not want anyone to get a whiff of her state of mind.

Gopa carried Riju to the sofa in Pinky's room. Pritha was sitting on the bed with Pinky and her son. She was playing with the baby. Look how quiet Bublai was in Pritha's lap! How surprising.

She couldn't possibly ask Pritha why she had come. Instead, Gopa put on a smile.

'You've come at the right time,' she said. 'Pinky arrived ten days ago. It's great that you can meet. Riju too hasn't seen his Pishi in a long time.'

'Mamoni, I dropped in because Pinky is here. And, of course, to see the baby,' Pritha said smiling cheerfully. 'Can you imagine! Our Pinky, a mother now? A responsible mother. I can't believe it. He's a beautiful baby, Pinky! So adorable. But look at his face! He's so miffed. Ha ha! He resembles his grandfather quite a bit, doesn't he?'

'Have you seen his grandfather?'

'Yes, of course, I have. He had come to see Pinky, remember? When the marriage was finalised.'

That was true. Seven years ago, Pritha had left home around this time. That was the reason why Pinky's wedding had to be postponed. Gopa remembered how hard it had been for everyone. During Pinky's wedding, the relatives had asked her about Pritha's whereabouts. She could not blame them. Pritha was her only son's wife, and it was indeed odd that she was missing from the wedding festivities. When Gopa told Bappa this he had been furious.

'Ma, this is entirely up to Pritha. She can leave whenever she wants to. It's her life. She left when she felt it was time to. What can she do if she doesn't want to live here anymore? Should she cry and be miserable all the time? Should she sacrifice her life? And why should she? Pinky's life won't come to a standstill because of Pritha. What does Pinky have to worry about? I'm here, aren't I? I will buy her the wedding Banarasi. I'll send the invitation card to friends and family. I'll tell them Pritha has left me, left us! Then no one will bother you anymore, right? I'll deal with them if they do. I have already told Pinky's father-in-law that Pritha and I are getting divorced. I don't know what he thinks of it, but it is going to happen. You get into all sorts of trouble because you hide the truth. No one has bothered me. I will answer everyone's questions. I don't mind.'

Pritha continued to call her 'Mamoni'. Gopa furtively sneaked glances at Pritha as she chatted with Pinky. She had not allowed herself to age, in fact, she looked younger than ever. There was no extra fat on her body. She wouldn't be surprised if Pritha was mistaken for a Bollywood starlet. She had always been glamorous, but there was something artificial about her appearance now. She couldn't spot any flaws. Everything was perfect. Yet, something was amiss. She did not feel overwhelmed in the presence of such beauty. What good was beauty if it did not have the ability to inspire or make you happy! All it did was stun you into silence like you were witnessing a magic trick. And stunned she was!

Pritha wore a pair of jeans and a linen shirt on her tall, slim body. Her throat was encircled with a brown and white cotton scarf. Her hair was arranged in a messy top knot. Gopa knew this was the latest fashion. As far as Gopa was concerned, this hairstyle looked like a bird's nest. Golden hoops as big as bangles, Pritha's trademark style, dangled from her earlobes. Her lips shone under a thick layer of gloss. Her nails were filed and painted white.

Her face glowed. The eyebrows were neatly shaped. There was a gold bracelet on her left wrist, while an expensive watch flashed on the right wrist. An ugly ring, a huge mother of pearl encircled with smaller pearls on a band of interwoven silver and gold, sat on her index finger. Bappa hated that ring. Gopa had no words for how ugly it was. Moreover, the massive ring looked especially out of place on Pritha's skinny finger. And most importantly, it looked extremely *cheap*. The ring alone was enough to ruin Pritha's otherwise elegant, sophisticated appearance. 'Please, Pritha, it's time to dump the ring. It turns me off,' Gopa had heard Bappa say.

'Wear it on your left hand if you must,' Gopa had said one day. 'You have such fine taste, but I can't understand your fascination with this thing!'

Pritha would never get angry. She did not heed their grouses at all. They had a family astrologer and none of them dared defy his instructions. It was he who had advised her to get a ring made of silver and gold. There was nothing she could do.

Pritha had studied at a convent school in Park Circus. She was smart and coquettish, spoke Bengali with a twang and heavily interspersed it with English words. She had complete faith in astrology despite being a staunch atheist. She celebrated Durga Pujo, but did not participate in any religious rituals. This was Pritha.

However, this was not all that Pritha was. She was born in 1980 in a well-to-do family in Kolkata, and like every child of that era, she received an English-medium education. Gopa knew this. After all, she used to teach History at an English-medium girls' school in central Kolkata. She left her job when she got pregnant with Pinky, many years after giving birth to Bappa. Still, it did not mean Pritha lacked gravitas. Gopa could not point to anything about her that she could *really* disapprove of. She could never bring herself to be angry with Pritha.

It was true her marriage with Bappa did not work out, but she had never picked fights with her mother-in-law. She had not ever misbehaved with Pinky. In fact, she was extremely fond of her. Yet, it took her only a moment to decide that she wanted to leave. Gopa had begged her to stay for Pinky's wedding. She was miffed about it for a long time. And she could not forget Riju. She had secretly blamed Pritha for the marriage falling apart. Then again, Gopa was known to be irrational when she was deeply hurt.

When things had settled down, she told herself that she was being unfair to Pritha. She could never successfully hold a grudge. It had been four years but she could not forget the day when Pritha had walked out with Riju in tow. A bitter feeling coursed through her blood when she was reminded how Bappa was prevented from seeing his son every day. Why shouldn't he see his son? Why should he be made to suffer? She could feel her heart beating madly. What right did this woman have to put Gopa's family through this?

She only had a vague memory of what Pritha said before she left. That plastic smile! 'Juhi was far more beautiful,' Gopa thought to herself.

'Ma, don't you want to know who this child is?' Pinky asked.

'Give me a moment, will you? I haven't seen Riju in ages. I can't take my eyes off him. How can I look at anyone else?'

Two years ago, Gopa had shown a similar politeness to Pritha. Even today she was very civil. She had not believed a day would come when her ex-daughter-in-law would visit her. No one had prepared her for this situation. What should she do and what should she say?

She sweetened her voice and cooed, 'Who's this? Who is this baby?'

The baby was playing on the bed.

'Boudi's son. He's just turned one,' said Pinky.

'You're already back in shape. I don't know how you do it! Yoga?' she turned to Pritha and asked. 'Meanwhile, I'm done for!'

Pritha's buttocks looked fleshier than before. Gopa averted her eyes and pulled Riju into an embrace once more.

'All in good time,' Pritha said. 'Don't worry about it. How long will you be here?'

'Six months at the very least.'

'I'm attending a crash course on post-natal health at Hyatt Regency next month. Seven days. Want to come? I'll sign you up.'

'Why not? Okay.'

'How did you know Pinky's here?' Gopa said. 'Did you know she had a baby?'

'Mamoni, I looked up Pinky on Facebook. I don't do it all the time though. But when I'm free, I look people up and see what they are up to. I didn't see anything related to pregnancy. She didn't post about it. Or perhaps the posts weren't set to public. A few days ago, Paramesh posted a bunch of photos of Pinky, himself and the baby. Pinky was tagged too. I was thrilled! I went through the comments and found out she was in Kolkata with you. So, I decided to visit. I spoke to Bappa yesterday and confirmed with him if she was indeed here.'

'Bappa and you are on speaking terms?' Gopa was surprised.

'Yes, yes. We speak all the time. For Riju.'

Gopa looked at Pinky, who immediately averted her eyes. As though she was silently trying to tell her mother not to to get into their mess. Pinky was always devoted to Pritha. Even now she addressed her as Boudi. Was Pritha still her sister-in-law? No, she wasn't. But Pinky still thought of Pritha as her own.

And yet, the woman who was her Boudi now, Juhi, was almost a stranger. They had never lived together in this house. Irrespective of what anyone said, Juhi was very sincere in her duties to the family. Yet, in these few years, Juhi had not become very dear to anyone besides Bappa. She was here just yesterday and had brought an armful of gifts for Pinky, who accepted them without any hesitation. But she did not ask about Juhi's well-being or chat with her. Pinky addressed her as 'Juhi-di', she refused to call her Boudi.

Gopa was aware that Pinky was still angry with her brother. Why did his heart bleed for someone else's son when he already had his own?

'Betus, Betus, my son Betus!' Bappa always went on.

Pinky could not stand it when her brother overdid his affection for Juhi's son.

'Riju is an angel. I don't see you going crazy for him. He's a descendant of this family. Pritha took him but you could have fought for custody. You are loaded! You did nothing and didn't get the law or courts involved. Doesn't it feel odd to you to marry a woman who already has a child? On top of that, you have no qualms about introducing him as your son to the rest of the world. You should have some shame,' Pinky often chided her brother.

Gopa had also not welcomed the situation. Therefore, she didn't visit Bappa's flat too frequently. He often invited his schoolfriends to dinner, sometimes with their parents too. Gopa had no choice but to attend those. But apart from that, she rarely had anything to do with them. She believed that they could do whatever made them happy but they should leave her be.

Bappa celebrated Juhi's birthday a few months ago. She did not attend the celebrations. Betus's school leaving exam results were announced a few days back, and Bappa celebrated it with yet another party. She sent a card and a box of sweets with Sukhen but did not go to the party. She simply could not celebrate with them. Her mind would always turn to Riju and images of him as a four-year-old flooded her mind. She must have seen him at least four more times since then. But she did not remember the intervening years too well. His face through the ages was becoming blurry.

Gopa breathed raggedly and sharp pain rose in her chest. She felt desolate.

Riju was Raibahadur Pramathesh Rai's grandson's son. He had a father who had a very well-paying job but he was being raised in a completely different household. It was obvious that Bappa was a far better man than the chap Pritha had subsequently married.

'Does Riju speak to Bappa?' Gopa asked as she stroked Riju's hair,

Riju looked at his mother and waited for her to intervene. Gopa could not gauge what was going on in his mind.

'I don't want to stop him, Mamoni,' Pritha said. 'But because of many reasons, the two do not meet very often.'

'But you said you speak to Bappa every day about Riju.'

'Bappa was drawing up his will. That's why for a few days …'

'Oh!'

Bappa was writing his will? And he was in touch with Pritha because of it? Gopa felt a heavy weight lift off her chest. This meant he still thought about his child and cared about him. At times, Gopa worried about how Riju had not enjoyed even a fraction of his father's wealth and that he might be cut off from his inheritance completely. In fact, she had often wondered whether only those who were presently living off Bappa would inherit all his wealth.

Mala entered the room with a trolley loaded with tea and snacks.

'You've brought food, Mala? What did you bring for my Riju?' asked Gopa.

Mala was an expert in these matters. She smiled in answer and got busy pouring tea. Juhi had brought an assortment of food yesterday. Mala had laid them out beautifully in plates and bowls. She even had shingaras delivered from Madan's shop. These shingaras, tiny but generously stuffed, were the shop's speciality. Gopa knew how famous they were. She liked serving them whenever she had guests.

'From Madan's?' Pritha exclaimed and grabbed a shingara. 'Remember when a business executive from Australia was visiting Bappa's office? He was completely bowled over by these shingaras!'

'Boudi, remember how he was blowing on them and chomping off one after the other?' Pinky added eagerly.

The two of them burst into laughter.

'Why was he here? I don't remember him,' said Gopa.

'Bappa was giving him a tour of north Kolkata and then the two of them ended up here. He polished off all the shingaras and afterwards couldn't walk at all!' said Pritha.

Riju looked at his mother as she spoke about the old times. They were all slowly feeling at ease. Pinky was visiting from

Mumbai, and the mother and son had always lived in this house. Gopa was happy to be surrounded by her children, daughter-in-law and grandchildren. It was as if Bappa would storm in at any moment and break up the party.

'Come on now. Get up. Get ready, we'll go out for dinner,' he would say.

Pritha and Pinky were talking animatedly. Gopa got up, waved at them and left the room. She made her way to her bedroom and opened the doors of the ancient wooden almirah. She took a silver jewellery box and extracted a man's golden bracelet. She pulled out another necklace and returned to Pinky and Pritha.

The bracelet and the necklace were very heavy. They were studded with gems. Bappa's grandfather's name, Ajitesh, was inscribed on the bracelet. These were heirlooms. It wouldn't be an exaggeration to say that they had been passed down for seven generations. Gopa had locked away the jewellery in different safes. Pinky and Bappa were entitled to some of it. A few days earlier, Gopa had put together the jewellery meant for her daughter. It was time for Pinky and Bublai to have them. She chose the bracelet from Pinky's share to give to Riju. Who knew when she'd see him again! She had been robbed of opportunities to pamper him.

She had indeed brought the bracelet for Riju but unease niggled at her heart. She did not hesitate and in fact, gladly gave away family heirlooms to Pinky. She knew her daughter had the right to it. And so did her children. Gopa had even made arrangements for the possibility of Pinky being the sole owner of these goods in case something went wrong between Paramesh and her. But Bappa could do whatever he pleased with his inheritance.

She was hesitant to give Bappa his share. Juhi would definitely lay claim to all the jewellery. Knowing Bappa, he would gladly hand over everything to her. That would be the end of it! Juhi would ensure that the treasures were passed down to her son. His son would in turn hand them over to his wife. That was the natural way, after all. If only Bappa had a child with Juhi! Then it would be an entirely different matter. There was no doubt that Juhi was a wonderful person. And cunning? She had plenty of it. Anirban was Bappa's friend. He was a loser. A complete loser. Juhi set her eyes on Bappa, a fresh divorcee, and kicked Anirban out of her life. She swallowed Bappa whole. The rest of the world watched on in silence.

She was afraid to give Bappa anything, but she felt a similar dread of giving Riju a share too. It would eventually end up in Pritha's hands. That would be the end! Who would assure her that Pritha would indeed pass on everything to Riju? She had another baby now. Was there any guarantee that Pritha would let Riju have what belonged to him? All this was too much for Gopa. Her thoughts had trapped her in a web of her own making. She did not wish to witness the family inheritance being squandered. She knew Bappa did not care two hoots about it. In fact, he had no idea of what his forefathers had accumulated and left behind. It was only Pinky who had her eyes on them.

Bappa's salary enabled him to buy expensive gems and jewellery, if he so wished. In fact, just last year, he bought a bag for Pinky from Italy, worth two lakh rupees.

'You could have bought gold instead, Bappa,' Gopa said.

'Many people live an entire year on this amount too,' Bappa answered coolly.

'My goodness, Bappa! You are a rich man, aren't you? You have so much money to throw around. Your father and grandfather were wealthy too, but your father, at least, was extremely careful with money. They wouldn't have survived if he wasn't.'

'Ma, what's the point of having money if you can't waste it every once in a while? I save a lot more than I spend. I'm into philanthropy too. You know how involved Juhi is in social work.'

She was wondering if she should give the bracelet to Riju.

'What's the younger one's name?' she asked Pritha.

'Rick.'

'Rick? Lovely! Raktim's brother, Rick. It's a nice name.'

She looked at the baby and smiled. The baby smiled at her widely in return.

'Daat! Daat!' he babbled.

'What's he saying?'

'Daant! Teeth! See, he's got a few tiny ones.'

'Does he have a grandmother, Pritha?'

Gopa could not stop smiling as she picked up the baby. She brought Riju close too.

'Take a photo!' she said to Pinky as the thought suddenly struck her. They did not take too many photos the last time Pritha was here.

Pinky took a bunch of photos on her iPhone. Gopa planted wet, noisy kisses on both boys. These moments were captured too. Like a greedy old fox, Gopa delighted in the fact that she now had many photos of her grandson. She would browse through them whenever she felt like it. Bappa would see the photos too. She would tell Pinky to send her the photos. She returned Rick to Pritha and embraced Riju once more.

'Do you really know who I am?' she asked him.

Why was Bappa's son so shy? His head was always lowered. Riju looked at his mother before speaking.

'Granny from father's side,' he said in crisp English.

That was all? Amazing.

'Would you like to stay with me for a few days?' Gopa asked. 'Your aunt is also here. She'll play with you. It's your summer holidays.'

'Mom won't allow it. I'll come tomorrow,' he answered in a mix of English and Bengali.

'When?'

'Who knows!' He looked at his mother once again.

Look at him! Gopa could not untangle herself from the web. Feeling desperate to break free, she did something completely uncharacteristic of her. She lovingly slipped the bracelet on Riju's wrist and handed the necklace to Pritha.

'This is for Rick. He's an angel. My heart is full. May he always be happy.'

Despite trying very hard to restrain herself, Pritha could not conceal the surprise on her face. She quickly rearranged herself.

'No, no, I cannot. Riju will get both, Mamoni,' she said.

Gopa felt Pinky's eyes on her but she decided to ignore her.

'I know you'd rather have everything to yourself. I was not against Betus getting some of it. You made me bitter towards him. Betus likes me quite a lot. He made me the chief guest during a dinner party where he had cooked the food. His friends dropped in unannounced and he had to go away with them. But how profusely the boy had apologised for it! I haven't ever felt any hostility from Betus. This incident happened two years ago but still ...' she thought to herself.

Perhaps, every human being is selfish. It made Gopa happy to think that whenever Riju thought about his 'granny from father's side', he would think of her as kind, a woman with a heart. That was all she wanted.

Gopa had never seen Pritha eat properly. She had lived in this house for a little over six years but she often refused what Mala served.

'There are fish cutlets. Will you have some, Pritha? Gopa offered despite everything, 'What about you, Pinky?'

'Why not!' Pritha exclaimed after a brief pause.

Gopa went to the kitchen in search of Mala. She was not there. Instead, she was in Gopa's room putting away freshly ironed clothes in the wardrobe.

'Fry some cutlets for Pritha and Pinky,' Gopa said in a low voice, standing close to her.

'Right away,' said Mala.

'Things that people have to agree to in the name of politeness,' Gopa muttered to herself. 'Can you ever honestly say what's in your heart? I don't think so! She won't let Riju visit, won't let him see his father, won't let him have a relationship with this family but she'll visit whenever she feels like it. Fantastic! Why is she here? We no longer have anything to do with each other. How can she drop in whenever she feels like it? What if I turn up at her house whenever I want to? Will she welcome me with open arms? My son has forgotten about his son. His head is in the clouds. This is what I have to live with!'

Gopa vented carefully in Mala's presence. She would definitely relay every word to Juhi. Pritha had turned up with Riju. Would Juhi not hear about it? Of course, she would. Let her! That was why Gopa thought it important to have Mala know her true feelings. She couldn't risk a misunderstanding.

She went back into Pinky's room after sending Mala off to the kitchen. The two women were still chatting.

'Pritha, I forgot to ask … how's your mother doing?' she said.

'She's in America with my brother. She won't come back till Pujo.'

Pritha had just finished speaking when Juhi parted the curtains to Pinky's room and walked in. She greeted everyone with a smile before slipping back into her regular, stoic expression. This did not escape Gopa's eyes. Gopa was startled to see Juhi and she did not know what to do at that moment! What new trouble was this! Speak of the devil and …!

'Come in, come in, Juhi,' she said nervously. 'You are having a grand time, I see,' said Juhi with a tight smile.

'Sit, Juhi-di,' said Pinky.

Pinky's face was a sight to behold. She was very fair and even the littlest discomfort instantly made her face red.

'I think I turned up at the wrong time. I wasn't expecting this at all!' Juhi said, trying her hardest to look embarrassed.

'What do you mean?' said Gopa. 'This is your home. You are welcome at all times. The things you say! This is Riju and this is his mother. Have you met Riju before?'

Gopa's voice dipped when she said 'your home' because she suspected Pritha would feel offended. But why should she! This was the truth. However, Gopa knew that in her heart of hearts, Pritha was still dearer to her than Juhi. She was Riju's mother, the mother of the next generation of the Rais. In this equation, Juhi was an outsider.

'No, I've never met Riju. Never got the chance to. But I have seen his photos,' Juhi said, looking at Pritha with steely eyes. 'On Facebook,' she concluded with a smile.

Pritha answered Juhi with an insincere smile. A situation that none of them had wanted was playing out before them. The ex and the current wife were in the same room. And Gopa was caught between the two.

'Senjuti, Shahana's sister, is my school friend from Patha Bhavan. Shahana also went to the same school as us,' Juhi settled herself on the sofa and added. 'Both of them are on my Facebook friend list. That's how I find out everything. Shahana was here last winter and both of you went to Hong Kong and Macao together. If I'm not wrong, your parents live with your brother now. We have many mutual friends on Facebook. For example, Archie and his wife Kaju. Their son is friends with my son. Since they were babies!'

Juhi fingered her necklace, perhaps to mask her anxiety and awkwardness.

Meanwhile, Pritha swung her hair across her shoulders and was patting it continuously. She banged her big toe against the sofa in front of her.

'Yes, I know Senjuti and you are childhood friends. Archie and Kaju live in the same neighbourhood as my parents.'

'The Ballaris?'

'Oh, Sheela Mashi! Is their surname Ballari?'

'Yes,' Juhi nodded her head.

'Sheela Mashi is my aunt's sister-in-law.'

'I know,' said Juhi.

Would you listen to that! What six degrees of separation? All of them already knew each other, some were even family!

Gopa cursed Facebook. Everyone was on it. Everyone kept tabs on each other. What they were up to, where they were, what they were eating, what the husband gifted his wife on their wedding anniversary, how much their kid scored in the exams, whose house was invaded by an army of monkeys … everything! Yes, yes, just ask Pinky! Around a dozen monkeys had turned up at one of her friends' houses. She posted a photo of the animals reaching for a mango from the other side of the window.

'What good will only one mango do? Do you know how hungry they are? You should have given more food to the cute babies!' someone had commented.

'How many mangoes would you have given, madam? Not even one, I'm sure. Isn't it natural to do good within one's means?' someone else retorted.

She and Pinky had laughed uproariously while reading the comments.

Gopa was lost in thought. All of this meant Pritha knew what Pinky was up to and Juhi was up-to-date with Pritha's life. Why did everything have to be so confusing? By the looks of it, everyone was under surveillance. Pritha and Bappa got divorced and moved on to their second marriages. In fact, one of them had a new baby too. What was the need to still lurk around in the lives of their former spouses?

Pritha had not given any indication that she too spied on Bappa and Juhi, but Juhi felt no remorse in admitting that she was well-versed in what was going on with Pritha. However, it had started to feel as though Pritha was not as innocent as she portrayed herself to be. Juhi was not snobbish like Pritha and perhaps that was why she did not hesitate to speak the truth.

Gopa had trouble sleeping and right now, she worried that these thoughts would keep her up all night. She was stuck with a puzzle that she couldn't solve. What did all of this mean? Surely it was no fun watching your ex's life unfold on Facebook when you were no longer married to them. In fact, it must be rather painful.

It did not sound as though Juhi, while talking to the woman who used to be Bappa's wife and the mother of his son, was at all interested in keeping herself digitally away from the mess of her husband's previous marriage. It did not seem as though she stopped to think to herself, 'No, there's no need for me to see this.' These days, no one seemed interested in firmly shutting the door on the past. Gopa couldn't fathom why. They always kept the door slightly ajar. It was not possible for her to understand these modern ways. But if she were in Juhi's place, rest assured, she'd not be snooping on her husband's ex-wife. No thanks, she did not have such morbid interests!

She remembered her friend Archana from her time at Bethune College. She got married to a rich divorcee, out of the blue, just a few days before graduating. Gopa visited her friend in her new home and found a huge portrait of the husband's ex-wife hung right above the bed they slept in. This made Gopa angry beyond reason. She got into a spat with Archana before walking out the door.

Gopa and Pinky were merely the audience now caught in a showdown between two divas. She imagined Pritha as Kareena Kapoor Khan and Juhi as Vidya Balan. Kareena might not be as tall as Pritha, but both boasted a lovely peaches-and-cream complexion. Whereas Juhi was exactly like Vidya, or at least, as plump as her. She had a schoolteacher personality, a lovely sight at the workplace and just as comely as a housewife. Juhi was draped in a floral-patterned jamdani saree. Her blouse was skintight with a plunging neckline. Her hair was in a topknot. Juhi had adorned herself with jewellery like she always did. Gopa knew that was how Bappa wanted it. Today too, she was covered head to toe in expensive jewellery. Diamonds shone on her earlobes, a necklace dotted with gems sank into her bosom, she wore a cuff along with bangles on her left wrist. Gopa also spotted a matching bracelet. Added to these was a wristband in deep purple. It was lavishly studded with gems too. Her fingers flaunted diamond rings. As you can imagine, her left hand was a sight to behold. Her right wrist was empty save a watch. Her lips were painted a dark colour. Despite her heavy-set figure, Gopa thought, Juhi certainly looked far better than Pritha. She did not like Pritha's sparse elegance.

Juhi exchanged a few words with Riju. She pinched his cheeks and ruffled his hair. She sat Rick on her lap and cooed at him. She seemed to be fonder of Rick than Riju.

'She is also your mother, Riju,' Gopa had almost blurted out. But she checked herself in time. This was an outdated thought. The father's wife was not necessarily the child's mother. Moreover, it would be rude to impose a new mother on a child who did not even know his own father very well. He would be confused and barely be able to contain his surprise. Every relationship was important, especially one between a stepmother and a child. Gopa felt even angrier. And sad too. Why did Pritha keep the child from his father? What a grave injustice! One day, Bappa and his son would become friends. And Riju would never forgive his mother for her wrongdoings.

'Why did you keep me away from him?' Riju would surely ask someday.

Would Gopa be alive to witness that moment? Perhaps it was only ten years away. Riju would be an adult then. His mother would no longer be able to keep him under her thumb. What did Pritha gain from robbing a child of his father's attention and affection? Now she also had another baby.

'Did you have the child all on your own, Pritha? Did the father have no role to play?' she thought.

Bitterness swelled in Gopa's heart. She felt irritated. Why did Pritha drop in unannounced? Such behaviour was out of fashion, was it not? If she was under the impression that she had a right to this house and its inhabitants because she was Riju's mother, then Gopa would tell her that she was sorely mistaken. Things would have been different had she remained single. But no, she got remarried only a few days after the divorce. Shameless! Juhi was much better.

As soon as she decided that Juhi was better, she felt conflicted about it. Better? How was Juhi any better? She had done the same too. She walked out of the house with her son and got married to Bappa without batting an eye. What became of the husband, her child's father, their family? She did not stop once to think about them. Did Juhi permit her son to see his grandmother?

Pritha and Juhi were chatting away merrily, though both hesitated to look at each other directly. There was no warmth in their chatter and yet! Gopa thought they were treating each other as strangers at a friend's house, where they had no choice but to make small talk. *How are you? Is that what happened? You wouldn't believe it, but the same happened to me too*. No real conversation. They looked at each other through the corner of their eyes. Pritha sneaked glances at Juhi when she turned away, and vice versa. This did not escape Gopa's notice. And these were not merely glances of appreciation. It was much more. But what exactly, Gopa couldn't say …

Pinky was now a part of this aimless conversation too.

'When did you arrive, Boudi?' Mala asked. She nervously scurried out of the room before Juhi could answer.

She turned up again with a cup and a small pot of tea. The three of them were chatting about the schools in the city, their curricula, academic pressure and how their children coped with it.

'I'm out of it! Thank God,' Juhi said. 'I can't tell you how horrible the last four years were. I mostly stayed out of the home this time around. His exams were looming around the corner but Betus spent all his time chatting online. I couldn't bear it. Bappa mandated that he would sleep with Betus at night and thanks to him, Betus had no choice but to study. Though I don't know how much studying he actually did!'

A sharp pain pierced Gopa's heart. Bappa had never bothered to keep himself updated on his son's academic progress. Poor Riju did not even grasp that the Bappa being spoken about was his own father. If only he was old enough to! He was still a baby. Who could blame him?

Bappa loved Juhi's son, cared about him and played an important role in his growing up. Pritha detected these facts from what Juhi said, but she did not exhibit any emotions. All of them were seasoned actors. Of course, this realisation had hurt her. As it would hurt anyone. But then, why should it? Pritha had taught Riju to address her new husband as Baba.

And what about his real father? Legally, he had no existence in Riju's life. Riju was no longer a Rai. He was now Raktim Mukherjee. Perhaps it was also true that Bappa and Riju no longer had anything to do with each other.

'Riju is in the fourth standard and I'm already losing my mind,' Pritha said. 'There's too much pressure. He always has tonnes of homework and projects. I don't know why! The projects are too complex for kids and it's the parents who end up doing them. Rick will start playschool next year. Meanwhile, Sammya is in Mumbai for almost the entire month. I'm thinking about moving there too. The younger one doesn't know what a father is, but my main concern is Riju. He's always sad.

'"Mama, it's no fun when Papa isn't around," he says. Mama, of course, is of no use to him! Mama starts chatting with different aunties wherever she goes, she can't play like Papa, wrestle like him or roar and bark like him! He takes Riju swimming with him! Riju has no confidence in his Mama. He's crazy about rifle shooting and blames me for not letting him join classes!' Pritha smiled widely.

Riju was listening carefully to his mother.

'But you promised!' he said.

Gopa sighed deeply as she realised Sammya loved Riju too. It was a great relief. This was how it was. Whatever had to happen had happened. It was done now. One could not go back in time. None of them had sworn to live their lives just for the sake of their children. As long as the children were not unhappy or neglected …

Had the definition of parenthood changed? Wasn't Gopa told that being parents meant unconditionally loving, caring and sacrificing for your child? As long as the children were happy and looked after …

Pinky was new to motherhood. It had only been a few days. Still, she did not want to be left behind.

'Indeed! My holidays will soon be over,' she added. 'A few more days and we'll start worrying about schools. I don't know how I'll manage if Paramesh is made to stay back in Dubai. Should I go back to Mumbai or move to Dubai …'

'No, why will you live there? You should go where your husband is,' Pritha answered and shook her head.

'There are many Indian academies there. They are very good. A child needs both his parents,' added Juhi.

'My goodness! Look at them! Devoted wives!' thought Gopa to herself. Maybe it took a divorce and a second marriage to be so devoted to the husband. She wished she could interrogate the two divas in front of her. Such an opportunity would probably not present itself again! Let it be. Her patience, envy, thoughtfulness and civility were being tested today. She should pass with flying colours.

Mala entered the room with a plateful of cutlets.

'Mala, why haven't you tied your hair?' Juhi asked. 'Don't you bathe in the evening? You should bathe by four o'clock and change your clothes. It's so hot! You should change at least three times in a day.'

'I was just about to shower!' Mala said, laughing. 'And all of you are here …'

'She's very punctual,' said Gopa. 'In fact, I'm sick of her nagging me to be on time! She has been trained very well.'

'Bappa's subordinate executive's wife had organised a maid training camp last winter. I sent my entire staff there. They had a great time too. I heard there was an outing of some kind. She's going to organise another camp this winter. I'll send Mala. You'll come to stay with us, Mamoni.'

There was clearly no restraint in the conversation anymore. The topics of conversation were changing at a dizzying speed. Gopa silently observed Pritha and Juhi. Her heart grew heavy with the realisation that she was not particularly fond of either of them. She was bereft of any feelings. A daughter-in-law was supposed to be dear to you. Yet neither of the two women was really her son's wife. They did not know how to honour this title. She had seen her mother, mother-in-law, grandmothers embody the roles of a dutiful daughter-in-law. They were the lifelines of the family. It was her ill-fortune that these two women were no one to her. She could not wait for them to finish their chatter and leave her alone.

The evening set in. The sounds of conch shells being blown in prayer filled the air. Mala rarely offered prayers at the altar in the mornings. But she never missed the evening prayers. The sound of the conch shell emerged from their house too.

'Time to go, Pinky. We met after so long,' Pritha said. 'I'm very happy, Mamoni. I'll leave now. I'll call. Take care. It was so nice to meet you, Juhi. Say bye to everyone, Riju.' Pritha prattled on as she readied Rick for the journey back home.

'Boudi ...' Pinky bit her tongue, corrected herself and continued, 'Pritha-di, I'll hold Rick for you.'

Khukumoni and Cheenu walked in through the door as if on cue. Gopa was growing tired of the surprises that the day was throwing at her. Just a moment ago, she was thinking about how what was unfolding in this room was nothing less than the plot of a melodramatic Bengali television serial. Now, with Khukumoni, even the cameo entry was taken care of. Gopa closed her eyes. But Khukumoni and Cheenu, the aunt and niece duo, were still there. In fact, they were staring with their mouths wide open.

'Well, well, if it isn't Pritha!' Khukomoni said, quickly regaining control.

'Pritha, my dear Pritha. Oh, my grandson, Riju, oh, oh,' Khukumoni, who had a habit of dragging out her words very slowly went on. 'Oh, who's this? Your son? Have you had another son? Isn't that wonderful! Everyone should have siblings. Plus, what would the new husband say! Ha, ha, ha! Oh Bordi, what kind of a mother-in-law are you? You didn't tell me anything. We spoke this morning! Pinky, did I miss the party?'

'Both your daughters-in-law are here,' she continued, turning to Gopa. 'Why didn't you say anything? Have you forgotten about me? Hold on, did you organise a prayer meet?'

'Sit, please. Hold your tongue now. Think before you speak,' said Gopa. 'I would have invited you if there was something. Plus, I'm so well-known for my religiousness, am I not?' Gopa was seething. Khukumoni was quite dense and did not mind anyone's admonitions.

'Bordi, what an exciting time in your house,' Khukumoni went on undeterred. 'Your daughter, two daughters-in-law, grandsons ...! I'm so happy.'

'I swear I felt something pulling at me ...,' she continued and hugged Riju tightly. 'I had to come here! That's why I brought Cheenu along. She readily agreed too. I haven't seen Pritha in ages. Maybe that's why my heart ...'

Khukumoni had clearly lost her mind. Gopa could not believe what she was hearing. Juhi must be getting angry too.

Hold on, hold on! What did she just say? Two daughters-in-law? Did Bappa have two wives? Stupid woman, a total fool!

Khukumoni was Gopa's cousin and Cheenu was her sister Ela's child. Khukumoni's mother was not right in the head. Khukumoni and Ela were not exactly mad but they were not sane either. Neither had control over their tongues, had little understanding of what to say when and did not know how to behave appropriately. Zero social skills, as they say. But they were extremely wealthy. And just as miserly too. The two of them were wearing sarees that were slightly better than rags. Ela got married but ran away from her husband's home while she was pregnant. She never went back. Khukumoni considered herself to be a real looker. She believed she deserved to marry a man settled abroad and she would work as a teacher there. However, no such man was interested in marrying her. Therefore, she had chosen to remain single. This was their story. Gopa loved them but could not stand to be around them for too long. Her uncle, aunt and Ela were all dead. The aunt and niece lived together and drifted in and out of their relatives' homes without caring for invitations.

'Khuku-mashi, you're still the same. Still so lively,' Pritha said. 'But I'm not your daughter-in-law anymore. Juhi is. Times have changed, Mashi. And Cheenu, how are you? What happened to the house in Beltala? I saw that a demolition was underway. Have you sold it off?'

'Yes,' answered Cheenu. 'Khuku-mashi and I have bought a big flat next door. There's a lift too. We have the terrace as well. The dogs stay on the terrace.'

Cheenu was exactly like her aunt. She had a thick tongue that hindered her speech.

'Everyone else is very upset about it,' Gopa said. 'The quarrels don't seem to end. They can't stand their happiness or anyone else's!'

'Ah, the dogs have a better memory than us humans. They are the best.'

'Cheenu, you've become so fat. Do something about it,' said Pritha.

'Give me your phone number, Boudi. I'll call you.'

'Yes, yes, give us your number. We'll visit you at home. I really want to, you know? I want to see your new home. I want to see my Pritha. No matter what, you were our daughter-in-law. See, I haven't forgotten you,' said Khukumoni.

'Give me your number, Cheenu,' Pritha said. 'I'll call you.'

Even after the exchange of phone numbers, Cheenu and Khukumoni were not ready to let Pritha go, 'Just a little longer, please.'

It's time to feed Rick. His nappy had to be changed too,' Pritha spoke curtly to the aunt and niece. Juhi was quiet throughout. The two fools had bumped into Juhi on rare occasions in this house. As was expected of them, they had very quickly cosied up to Juhi but today, their object of fascination was Pritha. More surprisingly, they seemed to be fonder of her now than when she used to be a part of this family. It was like the divorce hadn't happened at all! The court was not witness to these peripheral relationships and perhaps that was why the judges could deliver their verdict fairly.

Pritha never cared much about the aunt and niece, but still, she made it a point to honour these relationships. She had taken Cheenu shopping. To the dentist, too. She had even taken Khukumoni and Cheenu to her parents' home in

Dhakuria. Even after everything, she did not treat the duo any differently. Come to think of it, her relationship with Gopa had not changed either. It was not like they were ever extremely close. Did it mean that the only person with whom she no longer had a relationship was Bappa? A party had descended on her house and in this crowd, it was Bappa who was all alone. The rest of them continued to be how they always had been. Was Bappa really so unworthy of you, Pritha?

Gopa quickly brushed off her tears. Her grandson would leave at any moment. What if Pritha moved to Mumbai? Riju would no longer live in this city in that case. Her heart gave a sudden lurch, as though mocking her about her grandson's frequent visits while he lived in Kolkata. This house, with several storeys, one above the other, had many rooms. In front, there was a sprawling verandah lined with pink, green, white and black geometric tiles. It stretched from one end of the house to another. Juhi was still in the room. Bublai was on her lap. The rest of them had gathered on the well-lit verandah to say goodbye to Pritha and her son.

Gopa did not know what came over her.

'What about his poitey? We have to initiate Riju as a Brahmin, Pritha. It's okay if you don't want to, but Bappa might. I might too …'

Pritha was quiet. Gopa hugged Riju. 'Dadubhai, this is your house,' she whispered to him. 'You are its true owner. I'll wait for you to become a big boy. You come whenever you want to and till then, I will keep the house safe and sound. I haven't forgotten you.'

No one could hear Gopa. Riju turned his head and lightly kissed her cheek.

Pritha and Riju left right after. Juhi, who was usually loath to stay more than ten minutes, said her goodbyes after almost an hour today. Pinky had to breastfeed the baby.

The two fools, Khukumoni and Cheenu, had to leave her room and move the party to Gopa's instead. The old hag could not stop talking about Pritha.

'So, whose house are you going to tomorrow?' Gopa asked. 'You have plenty of gossip for them.'

'Shouldn't we?' Khukumoni was surprised. 'It's good news, isn't it? Pritha came here with her son. Wouldn't it be nice if things went back to how they were?'

'She visited us after two years. And went back to what? And with whom?' Gopa did not know what else to say.

She called Bappa later in the evening to tell him Pritha had been here with her son.

'Why? What happened? What did she want from you?'

'Hasn't Juhi said anything to you? She came to see Pinky's baby. Pritha too has another son. He's just turned one.'

'Is that so? Nice. Juhi is very introverted and she won't say anything even if she is hurt ...'

'Juhi? An introvert? Since when?' Gopa could not contain her surprise.

'You don't really know her, Ma.'

'Anyway, why should Juhi feel hurt?'

'No reason not to. There's no need for Pritha to be friendly with us.'

Gopa was shocked to hear Bappa speak.

'Your son was visiting his forefathers' house. If Pritha had any sense, regularly brought him over and allowed him to spend the night every once in a while, that should make you happy! He can't stay with you because some people might not like it, but he's always welcome here. You can be friends with Riju. But you have never thought about it, have you? Have you forgotten your own son?'

'If I suddenly become close to Riju, then Juhi and Betus will feel insecure. Moreover, Riju thinks of someone else as his father. I don't want to confuse him. We are two different families. We have been broken and pieced together several times. Your heart is in the right place, Ma, but I'm afraid you're not being logical. There's no need to repair burned bridges. It's perfect the way it is. Anyway, this is what it is.'

'And what about the house, the money, the inheritance?'

'Everyone will get an equal share. Juhi, Betus, Riju, Pinky, even Bublai.'

'So, your forefathers' riches will go to those who are not related to us by blood?'

'For how long have you enjoyed the riches, Ma? Are you related by blood?' Bappa could not stop himself from laughing. 'Think calmly about it, Ma. The inheritance does not just belong to one's flesh and blood. Outsiders have a right to it too. Just think about it and you'll know what I'm talking about.'

'Are Riju and Betus the same to you?'

'Perhaps not, but Riju's wife and Betus's wife will be the same to me.' Bappa laughed once again.

'You're too generous, Bappa!'

'Ma, it's all the same underneath. No ancestor can dictate who the real inheritor should be. What happened to Bikramjit anyway? You remember, don't you? His forefathers were loaded with land and money. He died all of a sudden from cancer.

Rani remarried. Now Rani's stepchildren live in Bikramjit's mansion. Anyway, I have to go now. I don't like talking about these things. I'll visit you the day after tomorrow. I have to call Juhi now. I haven't reached home yet. I don't want more complications in my life, Ma. It's time you understood that.'

It was quite late by the time Bappa finished the call. Pinky was asleep with her son. Gopa summoned Mala. The two of them scrolled through the pictures that Pinky had taken earlier in the evening. The tears that she had so carefully restrained till now gushed forth in a deluge. Not Pinky, not Bappa, not Pritha, and definitely not Juhi—at this moment, only Mala was her dearest, the only one she could call her own.

THE OLD AGE HOME

After finishing her shower at exactly ten o'clock, combing her hair neatly, lathering herself with moisturiser, and wrapping a crisply starched saree around her, Archana sat down in one of the three chairs lined on the verandah. This was her daily routine and she went about it like clockwork. No disruption today either. She held a book, a hand fan and a bottle of water in her hands. She lowered the bottle next to her feet. The sarees she wore were usually white or beige with colourful borders. Today, she wore an off-white saree with a black zari border.

Anima's eyes were fixed on Archana's feet. How beautifully she had pleated the saree! The sunlight illuminated her toes. It was the month of July and this time of the morning was very bright and hot. Anima sneaked a look at Archana from the corner of her eyes. Their complexions were similar. They were both dusky. However, a healthy diet and a comfortable life gave Archana's skin an enviable glow. On the other hand, Anima had turned ashen over the years, which she thought was better than being completely dark. Anima spent a few more minutes looking at Archana before turning her eyes to the chimney.

Anima stood at the far corner of the balcony where Archana sat. The dense shadow of the mango tree blocked out some of the harsh sunlight. Anima couldn't stand the sun. She was yet to take a bath. The bathroom would not be empty till eleven. It was a very busy time at the old age home, though the third floor was as quiet as ever. The buzz was on the first floor. That was where the kitchen was. The dining room too. As well as the men's quarters. A corner of the second floor was also earmarked for the male residents. The rest was occupied by the women, including all of the third floor. Those who were unable to climb down from the second and third floors were permitted to take their meals in their rooms. Each of them had a table by their bedside. Anima never went down to eat and neither did Archana. It had been only two months since Archana arrived at Maya'r Khyala, the old age home. Anima had been here for a year. She was sixty-five then and was a little over sixty-six now.

Archana was seventy, or so she had heard. Anima turned her eyes to the chimney once again. Seventy? Really? She looked much younger. No older than sixty! She still had an enviable figure. Archana had never married and therefore, she had not borne children either. If that was the reason for her taut body then why had Anima's gone to hell so quickly? She looked older than her years. Completely ancient. 'Hag! An old hag!' she thought to herself. Was it possible to taunt oneself? Still, Anima pulled faces at herself.

She remembered the Tapadars of her neighbourhood. How awful the young boys were to the old aunt! They would tease her relentlessly as soon as she stepped out of the house. The aunt was widowed as a child and she was as rude as she was quarrelsome. She would go around making mischief all day. It was widely known that she would throw dirty water on the passersby. Watching the old Tapadar aunt since she was a child, Anima feared that everyone became cantankerous with age. Or was it just the old aunt who had turned out this way? In her time, every house had half a dozen old people and each of them had a similar personality and all of them would get up to no good. In fact, she had three old people living in her childhood home. Her father's uncle, aunt and mother. All of them quite old. Anima was the youngest of her eight siblings, the runt of the family. She was prone to epilepsy spells and was kept out of school. When her siblings were at school and her aunts and mother were busy in the kitchen, she would spend her time with the oldies. That seventy-year-old man, was he any less of a pervert? He would lock himself in a room with her and show her all sorts of perverse things. Her mother had caught him once. No one could stop her as she ran to the kitchen, picked up a dirty broom and thrashed the living daylights out of him. It was the first and last time her mother had let her tongue loose without any caution. The next day, she was back to her usual, silent self. There was nothing more to say.

'We should have kicked the rascal out on the streets. He hasn't earned an honest day's living, forced us to look after him, and now, with one leg in the grave, he dares behave like a degenerate?' her aunt grumbled. 'My blood boils thinking what we have to live with. A good-for-nothing, a rascal!'

'Where will he go if we kick him out? Who will take him in?' another aunt added.

'No one will take care of him anymore,' her elder brother said. 'He can live in the room on the terrace. I will take his meals to him. This is how he will live till he dies. Why should we be forced to live with a man who is a pervert?'

Anima looked carefully at the chimney again. Seventy or seventy-two felt so ancient back then. Very, very old. Already tucked into their deathbed. How old were her father and uncles anyway? How old was she now? Was she ready to die? No, no! What had she even achieved in life …

She sighed to herself. All of this seemed like an elaborate facade if she took a careful look at it. She was so perfect, so well-behaved, such a goody-two-shoes, but what good had come of it? She was still kicked out of her house, wasn't she? She never married, suffered from bad health, lost all her siblings one by one, friends became strangers, strangers became the custodians of the house, and after negotiations and discussions, they decided that she no longer deserved to stay in the house. She was rid of. Were there old age homes in her father's time? Would anyone abandon them there? No, she didn't think so.

Anima looked at the chimney once more. She looked at it every day. Over the past eight years, she had gone from occasionally glancing to staring at the burnt brick chimney for hours on end. It must have been at least a few centuries old. No one knew the exact year when it was constructed, but it belonged to a British company. This factory was run by white men and batteries were made here. The rim of the chimney's mouth was still sooty. Even God had forgotten to note the last time the chimney was in use. And yet, the sun, rain and storm had left their mark on it. A banyan tree had crept out of it, and now its splendid canopy imposed itself against the sky. From where Anima stood, at least a mile away, it appeared as though the tree was standing proud in a vase. A sight to behold. The tree had grown so much in these few years. Anima looked at the tree. She could not tear her eyes away from it. Did anyone else spare a second thought for the chimney? She had formed a special bond with it. This small town was home to a famous university. In fact, the town was named after it. Two huge factories dotted the town's skyline. It was a pretty place, though very far from Kolkata.

Anima was still a stranger to the town. Then again, there was no need to become friends with it. Just because they had dumped her at the old age home, with bags and everything else, all those years ago, it did not mean the town was her home. Not at all. Anima pulled a face again. She imagined herself walking down the footpaths of Hatibagan after exiting Star Theatre with a small blue wallet in her hand, a colourful bag on her shoulder, wearing a black-and-orange saree. She examined the fares on display and haggled with the hawkers. She could buy a doormat or maybe a plastic flowerpot. Wouldn't a new saree be even nicer, perhaps another day! Today, a tender coconut would do or maybe, a chilled bottle of Fanta. Fanta!

She couldn't imagine herself as a day older than forty. The elders had stopped bothering her too much and she was free to do as she pleased. She was finally without a guardian! She was forty. The window of marriage was firmly shut now. It was long before the shrewd wives of the next generation would worm their way into the family. Anima had come into a little money. She was free to go wherever she wanted, whenever she wanted. No one worried about her if she returned home late. She did not know what had come over her but she had never experienced freedom like this before. This was the golden age of her life. Anima wanted to be forty forever. In her dreams, she still was. Fuck everything, she had no reason to think of this old age home as her own. She did not give a hoot about anyone here. Wasn't this place the reason for her losing her zest for life?

The years had added up, and Anima was no longer unaware of the new town she lived in. She knew its stories. They made their way to her ears even though she did not want them to. And there was Madhuri, who could not shut up to save her life. At other times, she would eavesdrop on Khokon and Madhuri's conversations. There was no dearth of ways to acquire knowledge here. The rumour was that the factory had been converted into housing quarters for workers but the chimney was spared from being taken down. A famous local contractor had converted the grounds around it into a garden. A boundary wall had been put up and benches were laid down all around. She had heard that the place was very beautiful.

Kajal-di lived on the third floor too in the room next to her. Once a month, she hired a rickshaw and went round the town. Someone or the other would accompany her on this expedition. She invited Anima, who always refused.

'No, no, no, I have no need to go out,' Anima said to herself. Why should she saunter around with Kajal-di? She was neither a friend nor family. They did not belong to the same class. Kajal-di had worked as a cook for more than forty years at a rich man's house in Delhi. She had amassed enough money by the time she retired. In fact, it was they who had made provisions for her to stay at this old age home. They still sent her money every month. Yes, Anima was indeed unwanted. Nobody in her family cared for her but that did not mean she should fraternise with the servant class. She came from a respectable family. The men in her family were doctors, engineers, lawyers and some had even completed their MBAs.

Anima was content with looking at the chimney from afar. She was at liberty to fantasise about it. She reminisced about visiting Delhi as a child with her father. At present, the chimney was as novel to her as the sights of Delhi, Lucknow and Agra. There was a lake nearby. It was a popular picnic spot. Anima had not been to the lake either. Just like she had fenced off Kajal-di's attempts to befriend her, she had also successfully stayed away from Archana, who had arrived at the old age home two months ago.

Khokon and Madhuri were devoted to Archana. She used to be a headmistress at a government school in this town. Everyone in her family was dead. She lived by herself for a few days after retiring but moved in soon after. She had an en-suite bathroom and had furnished her room with her own furniture. She had got a washing machine too. The rumour was that she was the highest-paying resident at the old age home; therefore, the staff doted on her and agreed to her every demand.

Khokon and Madhuri were always buzzing around her like busy bees, cajoling and coaxing her. Nothing was better than money! This was gospel truth. A plateful of fruits arrived for her in the late afternoon. She was treated to the best of everything as more days went by. She even made tea in her room. The water was boiled in the electric kettle. The laundryman took a load of her clothes every day. She only wore well-ironed sarees and had him wash and press her clothes.

In the evenings, Archana played music at a very low volume. Anima could identify the tunes of a sitar, xylophone, flute and the rhythm of kirtans. The windows were covered with beautiful curtains. They looked very soothing as they blew in the wind. In these few months, Archana had laid claim to her side of the verandah. The other two chairs remained unoccupied. She didn't talk with anyone and went into town three to four times a month. Khokon would arrange a rickshaw for her. Archana would put on a pair of sunglasses before going out. She returned with her arms laden with biscuits and snacks from expensive shops. She had a small flat in Kolkata. Khokon had its spare keys. He'd accompany her to the city when she fell sick and needed treatment. Apparently, Khokon, Madhuri, Noni and Sarala got generous tips from her at the end of every month!

The men of the old age home neither cared about nor minded this arrangement. They were too old anyway and had resigned from life's petty politics a long time ago. However, the women had a hard time accepting the new order. They just could not stop talking about the newest resident. Their noses, instead of being on their faces, were in Archana's business. For instance, Sabitri-di, who was half-deaf and nearly eighty, was in great turmoil about this. Her home was somewhere deep inside Garia, in Fartabad. All of her children had stopped asking about her. No one could remember the last time they had visited her. They honoured their obligations with phone calls, which were few and far between. She was quite deaf, yet none of her children could be bothered to get her a hearing aid. They sent her eight thousand rupees every month and that was it. This paid for a shared room, a breakfast of tea and biscuits, two rutis, vegetables, one banana, one kalakand or a fistful of bonde. A bucket of hot water in winter. A lunch of two vegetable dishes, daal, fish and chutney. A cup of tea in the evening, followed by a snack of muri and chanachur. On some days, a treat of vegetable pakoras instead. A dinner of ruti and vegetables. During the season, a mango a day or an occasional piece of ilish. Goat meat once a month. There was chicken every Sunday. Boiled eggs at an additional price. Extra cups of tea if needed, also at an additional cost of ten rupees a cup.

Once or twice a month, Anima would ask for an egg roll. However, in this blasted town, neither the phuchka nor the egg roll was up to her standards. Her bowels often gave way the next day. She reminisced yet again about those happy strolls through College Street and the delicious moglai porota that was served on every corner.

Anima looked at the chimney again. Did the heart crumple with age? She looked at the skin of her arms. It looked like the scales of a sickly fish, dull and ashen, as though someone had carved hasty lines on her arms. There were countless wrinkles on her face.

The shadow of the mango tree swayed with the breeze. Birds cooed. 'No, Anima, the heart does not crumple with age. It is ageless,' she mumbled to herself. Anima's likes, tastes and interests had remained the same over the years. Ah, if only she had an en-suite bathroom with her room! She'd have the complete privacy to undress herself. And that song by Aarti Mukherji? She would sing it to her heart's content. Her voice was rather lovely. Surely her age wouldn't have turned her into a shrieking banshee? This was not a matter of flesh and bones that would decay with time. One could sing at any age. She could still sing melodiously with all the coquettishness of the film songs. She was not so old that singing anything besides devotional songs would seem offensive. For God's sake, she was only seventy-three!

Archana was always reading Rishi Aurobindo's or Swami Vivekananda's books in addition to Kaliprasanna Sinha's *Mahabharata*. Let her read them to her heart's content. It did not mean Anima should do as Archana did. Anima wished she had her spectacles with her. She would have liked to read novels like Bimal Mitra's *Kori Diye Kinlam* or Sankar's *Koto Ajanare* on the balcony. She wiped her face on her saree.

'Don't your legs hurt? You are always standing,' Prabha-di asked, placing a hand on her shoulder and interrupting her thoughts.

'Are you seeing me for the first time?' Anima lifted her face slightly and answered.

'Why don't you sit?'

'I can't till I have my morning shit.'

'I know.'

There was nothing this old hag didn't know. She kept glancing at Archana while she chatted with Anima. Prabha-di was married into a rich family. Her home was in Baranagar. The first time she spent a night outside her house was at this old age home. She arrived a few days after Anima. My God, how the old hag had cried! Wailed, rather. Not just from sadness but fear. She was so afraid that her face had turned blue. She was tall and wore nothing besides white sarees. She hunched a little and skipped when she walked, and her nose was in everyone's business. She had very strong opinions about every resident. Some tolerated her while others couldn't stand her.

It was just like being in a joint family. Everyone did not always get along. Was this not true for siblings too, despite having been born of the same mother? They held grudges and ill-will. Gossiped behind each other's backs. Maligned each other. Quarrelled amongst themselves. Abandoned or neglected one another. Went as far as trying to remove the others from their paths. It was the same here at this old age home.

Prabha-di could not walk without skipping, and thus, no one could hear her moving about the place. So, Chapala-di and Debi-di called her a ghost in secret. Apparently, such sly movements heralded bad luck. Nothing good ever came of it. That was the reason why she lost her husband at a young age and was afflicted by all the tragedies that followed. Oh, fuck all that! Anima thought to herself and pulled a face.

The rest of them didn't look in the mirror, did they? What about Chapala-di? What happened to Debi-di? All of them had very different, eventful lives. Debi-di took shelter at an ashram after her son-in-law kicked her out of the house. She somehow managed to sell the house and, with her share of the money, rented a room here and paid for her expenses. And Chapala-di? Her husband was sentenced to prison for rape and murder. She had to toil like a mule to raise her children and they did not care about her anymore. Her husband was still alive but she preferred to call herself a widow. And no matter where she went, the past caught up with her. Even here at the old age home.

Kajal-di, who had slaved at other people's homes all her life, was the most vociferous among them to have Chapala-di expelled. Latika, too, had started to sing her tune. She was a graduate and used to work at a bank. She was a few years younger than Anima. What a pandemonium! Everyone was after Chapala-di's life. But why should she leave? Chapala-di wasn't entirely innocent either. She had given a lot of trouble to some of the residents. The tears streaming down her face or her sorry past could not undo this now.

Meanwhile, Khokon became a staunch supporter of Chapala-di's. 'She has the right to stay here as long as she pays. Those who feel dishonoured by her presence are free to leave,' he declared. Everyone shut up right away. Still, it did not stop them from misbehaving with her in private. Then one fine day, things went back to the way they were and everyone was friends with Chapala-di again. She was back to her old tricks too. Forming cliques. Harassing others. The works. Anima Rai preferred to stay out of all this. However, she could not deny that the old age home had changed her.

Fish! Pieces of fish! This was the favourite topic of argument at the old age home. Anima had never imagined herself picking fights over food. She did not wrestle with pigs. However, was it possible to silently bear the humiliation of eating the fishtail or a similarly inferior piece for five days in a row? Surely, she could not stay quiet if they refused to give her hot water for her hot-water bag in winter, while her neighbour got it without even asking for it? Anima looked at the chimney again. Prabha-di had not gone away yet.

'Khokhon and Madhuri are arguing downstairs about their shares,' she lowered her voice and said.

'I can hear it.'

'Go downstairs and take a look. They are going at it. No control on their tongues ...'

'What are they saying?'

'The things they've got, the things they've asked for ... The old Samanta lady has died, and under her bed ...'

Anima saw Archana get up and make her way to her room. She was classy. She was a retired headmistress. Perhaps she did not like idle gossip. Anima could not stand it either. She did not even like living among so many old people. Was there no old age home in all of this damned world where even the young lived? Everyone had one leg in the grave, yet there was no end to their greed or selfishness and they all conspired against each other. Such lowly behaviour was simply unbearable to her. Was it not possible to go back to being a forty-year-old, even if for two days? So, what if she wasn't married, so what if she had never married and was a virgin, so what if she didn't have a family of her own or any children? It did not matter that she never had enough money, that no one really cared about her, that she was not respected by anyone, that everything that belonged to her could be lined up on the rickety wooden shelf beside her bed. Little by little, she was kicked out of the world and thrown into this rotten dump. No one asked after her. Apparently, her youngest brother's son had even paid Khokon in advance for the rituals that would have to be conducted upon her death.

And yet, life brought great joy to Anima. All she desired was to live her best years just one more time. For instance, that one time when she went off to Gariahat without telling anyone, riding alone in a taxi. She returned after buying a white nightie with black flowers and a housecoat. It was a different matter that she felt too awkward wearing it in her nephew's presence. She packed it with herself before coming here. The nightie was twenty-five years old but it was still in pristine condition. Apart from the waist straps that had come undone on the first day, the rest of it was still perfect. She wore it here for two days but everyone had ogled at her! Needless to say, the nightie was immediately packed up again. Sukhen-babu used to live on the first floor back then.

'So you used to be a working woman?' he took a good look at her and asked.

'No. Why do you ask?'

'Working women wear clothes like these because they're always so busy. That's why I thought you were used to dressing like this ...'

'No, nothing of that sort. I just have a few clothes like this ...'

'You're very modern.'

'Who are you to talk to me in this way?' Anima had huffed and gone into her room.

Sukhen-babu had fainted in the bathroom once and since then, he was prohibited from locking the door behind himself. Three-quarters of his life had gone by and he was staring death in the face. Still, it did not stop him from being rude to a woman.

Prabha-di was blabbering away when Anima suddenly started to feel nauseous. These days she spent a lot of time in the bathroom. Unnaturally long hours. The reason was constipation. It had got worse with age. She spent a lot more time in the bathroom than she did when she arrived here eight years ago. Thanks to the schedule that Khokon had drawn up, the bathroom would not be available to her before eleven in the morning. Everyone was old here and holding on when nature called was impossible. There were two bathrooms on the third floor and a room with an en-suite bathroom which was occupied by Archana. Anima could climb down to the second or first floor to empty her bowels but it would be afternoon before she would find an empty toilet. The queue for the bathroom was most intimidating in the morning. The residents lined up for the toilets once again after they were finished with their lunch. Anima had no appetite for jostling, so she had taught her bowels to control themselves. She had become quite good at it too. However, for the last few days, she felt uneasy after ten o'clock. A sharp cramp ripped through her belly. Walking became difficult and she could not sit either. Sweat leaked out of every pore and she experienced discomfort like never before. There were still twenty minutes to eleven. Anima clenched her teeth together and hoped the pain would soon pass. It did not.

She was annoyed with herself.

'What's wrong, Anima? Why does your face look like that?' Prabha-di asked. 'Hey! Hey!'

Anima held on to the railing tightly; she could not bear the humiliation, disgust and guilt coursing through her. She was about to do something that was completely unbecoming of her. Her face puffed up grotesquely as she tried to hold her breath. Her forehead felt clammy to the touch.

'Khokhon! Madhuri!' screamed Prabha-di. 'Where are you? Come quickly. Anima doesn't look well. Looks like she's had a heart attack!'

Anima's knees buckled and she fell to the floor. Still thinking of herself as a sprightly forty-year-old, she held on to dear life. A crowd had gathered around her by now.

'What's going on? What's this? How are you feeling?' Khokon asked.

'Bathroom,' Anima whimpered and pointed her finger at it.

Madhuri and Noni tried to lift her. Khokon ran off to empty the bathroom. She heard him banging on the door. She could not take it anymore. A moment longer and she would faint. Drool leaked from her mouth. Without wasting time, Khokhon went to Archana's room.

'Anima-di needs to use your bathroom. She's not well.'

Anima grabbed Madhuri and her arms flailed helplessly as she tried to make her way to Archana's bathroom.

'Oh God, have mercy. Don't humiliate me like this,' she muttered to herself.

'No, I won't let anyone use my bathroom,' Archana said, breaking her silence. 'Take her downstairs. Why my bathroom? What's the point of having a separate room if my bathroom is free for all?'

'I'll clean your bathroom, Didi.'

'I don't care. Go away, all of you. I'm not used to all this.'

'Why are you being so inconsiderate? She's the same age as you.'

'I don't care. Haven't I already said no? Am I paying so much for all of you to shit in my toilet?'

'Shut up! Don't go on and on about money!' Khokon lost his temper and shouted. 'I'm running this old age home for twenty years. I've seen plenty of vulgar folks like you. You are paying us to wipe your bottom in your old age—nothing more, nothing less. I pity you.'

'How dare you talk to me like that?' the former headmistress screeched like a woman possessed. A shrill and intolerable sound. Kajal-di flew to her side and yanked her away from the crowd.

'My God, how can someone be so cruel? Spick-and-span from the outside but entirely rotten inside!' exclaimed Debi-di.

A wave of joy washed over the crowd as they stood united in their resentment for Archana. Anima dashed into the bathroom. Meanwhile, the residents of the lower floors had also hobbled their way upstairs. Anima could hear everything from the toilet.

'I won't stay here another minute,' screamed Archana. 'Give me the keys to my flat. Call a taxi right away. Return every rupee from my deposit. Have I not paid you enough? Have I not fulfilled all your wishes?'

'Okay, okay. Go on then. Get lost. The room won't be empty for long. Ten others will queue up for it. And why won't you shut up about money? You don't own us.'

'I have slaved like a mule for you. Don't give me this bullshit,' screamed Madhuri.

From the toilet, Anima could hear Kajal, Chapala, Debi, Prabha, Sabitri and Latika speaking in unison. It was too late for a shower. She would lay down on her bed instead.

'Should I call for a doctor?' asked Khokon.

'No, I'm alright.'

'Let me know if you need a doctor. All of you think I only care about money. But that's not true,' he added. 'Understood, you old hag?'

'Hey, don't call me an old hag,' muttered Anima. 'I'm Anima. Why would you call me an old hag when my parents have given me a perfectly good name?'

'Oh! That's rich coming from someone who just shit her pants!'

Anima turned her face away in anger and embarrassment.

'Just see what I do if you ever bring it up again!'

Khokon laughed and left the room.

Archana went out in the afternoon. She did not eat lunch. It was eight in the evening when she returned. Madhuri followed her bearing a cup of tea.

'Madam Headmistress, have some tea. Don't be angry. These things happen when so many people live together. Khokon-da has made Maggi for you. Have some.'

After a few more minutes of coaxing, Archana finally opened the door and accepted the tea.

A few more days went by.

Archana did not leave. Khokon brought kachoris and sweets for everyone one day. The residents were inside watching a television serial.

'It's the headmistress's birthday. This is from her,' said Madhuri as she distributed the food.

Chapala-di and Debi-di looked at each other as they stuffed their mouth with kachoris.

'There's tea too. Noni is making it. Dig in, everyone.'

Noni winked at everyone in the room.

'Call me a rickshaw in the evening,' Anima told Khokon one day. 'I want to see the chimney up close.'

Kajal-di wanted to tag along too. Anima dressed up in a green and brown saree, and with Kajal-di for company, set out to see the town. For the first time in eight years.

AN ASHOKA CENTRE FOR TRANSLATION SERIES

This new translation series introduces English-language readers to some of the best Indian works of fiction, both modern and classic, that have sustained a wide readership in their source languages. Selected by the respective translators and co-published with Westland Books, the titles in this series are being presented by the Ashoka Centre for Translation as part of its commitment to foster India's multilingual ethos.

To find out more about the Ashoka Centre for Translation's initiatives, please log on to translation.ashoka.edu.in.